West Wind Calling

Carolyn Pogue

West Wind Calling

Carolyn Pogue

Sumach Press
Toronto

Gwen: West Wind Calling
Carolyn Pogue

First Published in 2012 by
Sumach Press, an imprint of Three O'Clock Press Inc.
180 Bloor St. West, Suite 801
Toronto, Ontario M5S2V6
www.threeoclockpress.com

Every reasonable effort has been made to identify copyright holders. Three O'Clock Press would be pleased to have any errors or omissions brought to its attention.
Three O'Clock Press gratefully acknowledges financial support for our publishing activities from the Ontario Arts Council, and the Government of Canada through the Canada Book Fund. We acknowledge the support of the Canada Council for the Arts which last year invested $20.1 million in writing and publishing throughout Canada.

Library and Archives Canada Cataloguing in Publication

Pogue, Carolyn, 1948-
    Gwen : west wind calling / Carolyn Pogue.

(Gwen ; 2)
ISBN 978-0-9866388-7-9

    I. Title. II. Series: Pogue, Carolyn, 1948- . Gwen ; 2.

PS8581.O2257G943 2012   jC813'.54   C2012-903088-0

Cover photograph: Copyright 2012 © Dr. Farook Oosman
Illustrations: Ben Craft

Printed and bound in Ontario, Canada by: Webcom Inc.

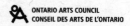

This book is dedicated to Janie Williamson and to Cadence, Foster, James, Kate, Michael, Tristan and Willie

Dear Reader,

I am descended from a heroine. No one remembers her, likely, except her grandchildren and great grandchildren. But when she was a little girl, she had to be very brave.

Like children around the world today who get caught in poverty or other difficult circumstances, Gladys Gwendoline Parsons had to be smart and brave in order to survive.

This book and the one before it, *Gwen,* honours the courage and resourcefulness of kids, past and present.

I also wanted to honour the creativity and courage of one of Canada's early writers, E. Pauline Johnson. At a time when women couldn't even vote, and were expected to get married and raise a family, Pauline Johnson chose a different path. She travelled the US, England and Canada for years and performed her own poetry. She published fiction and nonfiction for adults and children. Writers in Canada today, especially women writers, owe her a debt. Pauline is a heroine of mine and, as you will see, Gwen's heroine, too.

Because part of this story is based on fact, though most of it is fiction, I have included some notes for the curious at the back of this book.

I hope that you will learn more about the real 100,000 British Home Children who came to Canada to work as servants and farm hands. You may visit Peterborough, Ontario, to see the beautiful monument erected in 2011 which honours the many thousand who arrived there from Britain and were then sent out to work. The original home, Hazelbrae, has been torn down, but you can see the grounds and visit the church that the children attended.

I hope you will also explore the life and work of E. Pauline Johnson. You may travel to Six Nations Territory near Brantford, Ontario, to visit Chiefswood, the Johnson family home, now a national historic site.

May we all remember the children, and work for a world where every child is safe and loved.

Carolyn Pogue

Calgary, Alberta

2012

A glimpse of *Gwen*, the first novel

On the night of Gwen's 10th birthday in 1895, her father (a janitor in a London theatre) sneaks her backstage to watch an amazing performance by Mohawk poet E. Pauline Johnson. Gwen determines that she must learn to read and write so that she can grow up to be just like Pauline Johnson. She imagines Canada to be a beautiful, faraway land because Miss Johnson paints such a pretty picture of her homeland.

On Gwen's 11th birthday, her dying dad gives her a copy of Pauline Johnson's book of poetry, *White Wampum*. Orphaned, Gwen is taken to a Girls' Home, trained as a servant, then shipped out to Canada to work. Here, her adventures take a different shape.

West Wind Calling begins on Tuesday, February 15, 1898, when Gwen is 13.

Funerals

The funeral is hard. First, they carry in one big, wooden coffin with Mr. Brown's body in it, and then the little tiny white coffin for baby Reg. Father and son.

Even the minister has tears on his cheeks. When we sing *Unto the hills around,* I lift up my longing eyes, which is a Bible song, Molly's family sings *Se wen ni io saw entsi,* which is the same, but in the Mohawk language. Mr. Brown would have liked that.

My belly is a solid knot. I don't want to scream. I don't want to think too much about how this is like, but not like, the funeral for my own dad on my eleventh birthday, May 4, 1895. It was three years ago in London. That's in England.

The air is thick with the smell of flowers. Someone must have collected every living flower in Ontario and brought them here. At my dad's funeral, the only flower was the one that I picked up off the street after it fell from a flower cart. I pinned that limp pink rose on his best jacket for his burial. I thought it looked pretty dandy.

At my dad's funeral, it was hot. The gravediggers waited, sweating by an oak tree, wanting us to hurry so they could go home or maybe up to the pub for a quick pint. But at this funeral no one's in a hurry at all. At this funeral, it's cold. Cold to walk behind the horse-drawn hearse from the house to the church. Cold to walk behind it to the cemetery and stand by those deep, dark holes while the minister God-blesses us and says thanks for the lives of Mr. Brown, a very brave man, and little Reg, not two years old. Cold to stand still while Mrs. Brown grips my arm like a vise and stands like a statue, like a stone angel maybe, and stares into a future that she has to walk into alone.

I don't see a gravedigger anywhere here. I recognize all the people at the grave, except two men, and they aren't holding shovels.

It isn't right at all. I know that sometimes grownups die. Mum died when I was five, then Dad. That's how I ended up in The Girls' Home and got trained as a servant. But it's not right for a mother to have to watch that little coffin go down into that hole.

On my eleventh birthday, Dad gave me a copy of *White Wampum,* Miss Pauline Johnson's book of poems. Then, his breath rattled around in his chest, and then he died. And after we buried him with all the rest of his stories still inside him, our neighbour, Mrs. Bostwick, marched me straight back to our little fleabag flat. While I was making plans to run away and be a lady in the theatre, she was dragging a man through the door who told me he would not take me to the workhouse, *nosir,* he would take me to a special Girl's Home, and after I was trained, he'd maybe send me out to Canada to be a servant, and he did.

And so now I am shivering beside the double grave in Brantford, Canada, and ready to go back to the Brown's house and serve all the little sandwiches I made with the neighbour ladies and pour the tea and serve little pastries that I made at 6 o'clock this morning. And so this funeral is exactly the same as my dad's and not the same at all.

"We commend these, your children, to your everlasting arms,

Almighty God," the minister says. And the people say, "Amen," only I don't because if God is really Almighty, maybe Mr. Brown wouldn't have been beaten up. And maybe he and little Reginald would not have died from influenza. What about that, God, I wonder. But then, maybe "Almighty God" doesn't mean that people you love never get sick or beaten up or die. Maybe "Almighty God" means One who can think up how to make bears and rivers and trees and the rest is sort of up to us?

I would like to talk to Mr. Brown about this, but he's dead. I would like to speak to Maggie about this, but she is still a House Mother at the Home in England. I would like to talk to Tim, my best friend from England, but he's out in the Northwest Territories now. I suppose I could talk to Molly's grandma on the Reserve, but without Mr. Brown here, how will we buy feed to keep the horses to pull the carriage all the way from town to the Reserve?

When the last Amen is said at the grave, we get into the black funeral stagecoach and drive slowly back to our house. The four black stallions have black harness plumes to show respect for the dead.

Mrs. Brown hasn't let go of my arm yet. She must be thinking that if she lets go of me, she might fall apart or drift away. It's the least I can do for her, be an anchor. I might be a servant, but I know that Mrs. Brown likes me. She even calls me "dear." So I don't mind being her anchor on this tragic day.

We drive through cold streets, under naked trees to our sad

house with the black mourning wreath on the door. We stop in the front hall where the mirror is covered with black cloth. Mrs. Brown doesn't seem to know what she's supposed to do next. She just stands there, so I take her hand gently and, one finger at a time, take off one black leather glove and then the other, while she stands staring at the staircase. In the part of the staircase where it bends, there is a grandmother clock *tick tock tick tock*. In the sadness of the day, the clock seems very loud.

The coffins were in the dining room for two days, so the furniture had been moved against the wall. That way, people could come, take a look and say goodbye to baby Reg and Mr. Brown. Now I see it's all been moved again so that people can visit and tell stories.

As people arrive and see us standing in the front hall they move around us the way the Grand River moves around a rock, just flowing gently to one side and the other. I remove Mrs. Brown's hat and coat; it's like undressing a statue or large doll. I take her cold, white hand, and lead her into the sitting room. "Alright Gwen, I'll sit with her while you see to the tea," says our neighbour Mrs. White. It's shocking to see Mrs. Brown like this, with all the colour and voice squeezed out of her. But when your son and husband die, that's what you look like.

In the kitchen I tie on my long white starched apron with the frills. My best friend Molly puts on an apron, too, even though she's not a servant. "I'll help you," she says, and picks up a plate of butterscotch squares and surges into the crowd with me. Fragments of conversation float toward us like ragged, wispy clouds.

"…no family I know of…"

"He was a courageous man, a hero…"

"She'll have to sell the house…"

"…catch the other two culprits?"

"…send the Home Girl back …"

I didn't like the sound of that Home Girl comment, but back in the kitchen Molly hugs me. "Don't worry, Gwen," she says. "Things will work out." I hope she's right.

~

That night, I lie in bed listening to Mrs. Brown slowly walk through the house. The glow of her lamp casts a feeble reflection up the stairway as she walks from the sitting room to the kitchen to the entrance hall, then up the stairs past that loudly ticking clock. She goes into the nursery, and I hear the rhythm of the rocking chair, sounding just like it did when little Reg was teething. Back and forth. Back and forth. It fills the house with longing and sadness.

She walks past my bedroom into her own lonely room. Weeping sneaks out from under her door and floats into mine. After a while, I tiptoe down the hall, open her door and climb into bed with her. Without saying anything, she moves over, reaches for my hand and falls asleep. But I don't sleep. My mind is on fire wondering what will happen, and darting between my life here and my life back in England.

My old dad was a cleaner at a theatre in London. One day, he sneaked me backstage so I could watch Miss Pauline Johnson's *breathtaking performance*. Miss Johnson is a Mohawk woman and a real Canadian, not like some people I've met since I arrived here just over a year ago. After I saw her, I made my friend Tim teach me how to read. I also decided to become a performer and go on tours all around England and Canada like her. I planned then to be a star in my own play; for example, "London Orphan Bravely Sails to Canada and Becomes Sought-after Performer."

My first placement as a servant in Canada was awful. I will likely have to make up a play about that, too. It would be called, "Orphan, Placed with Spoiled Girl, Fighting Family and a Very Bad Man, Triumphs Over Adversity," or something like that.

But the Home next sent me to the Browns here in Brantford, and they didn't make me eat in the kitchen all alone and were never mean to me, not once. I even made friends here, Molly and William, and I got to go to their farm on the Six Nations Reserve and stay for whole weekends. The Reserve is where Chiefswood is, where Miss Pauline Johnson lived when she was a little girl, and where she began writing stories and poetry.

If these last weeks were a story-poem in Miss Pauline Johnson's book, instead of my real life, it would be called, "London Orphan Bravely Sails to Canada, Only to Become Caught in a Heart-Breaking Situation." Maybe I will write that poem someday myself. But now I feel too sad. For a long time I lie in the dark and wonder what will become of us.

Leaving

Other people got influenza in Brantford, but they didn't die. I guess Mr. Brown was too weak to fight the illness after he had been beaten up. It was because of timber. People didn't like it when he went out to the Reserve for meetings about stopping the timber thieves.

Only a week before the beating, our neighbour Mr. Andrews came to visit. I was serving raspberry tarts and tea. "Mark my words," Mr. Andrews warned, "timber is money. You're dealing with powerful men. If you interfere, you might get hurt."

"But it's not right," Mr. Brown told him. "People from town are cutting Reserve timber and selling it right here in town. It's stealing."

Mr. Andrews was a big man, much bigger than Mr. Brown. He shifted his body on the chair and tapped ashes from his pipe into the glass ashtray. He fiddled with his watch fob and then peered over his spectacles. "I'm just saying that it could be dangerous. There's liquor sales involved, too, you know that. Bad combination, I'd say. Best to stay out of it."

But Mr. Brown didn't stay out of it. And then one night he was pulled out of his sleigh, beaten up and left in a ditch. Molly's dad saw the horse and sleigh standing on the road and went to see what the problem was. He found Mr. Brown bleeding nearby and brought him home to us. The police came, and Mr. Brown said that four men had attacked him. Molly told me later that it was like what happened to Chief Johnson in the olden days, and it was for the same reason—illegal liquor sales on the Reserve and illegal timber sales in town.

The police arrested two of the men trying to escape to Hamilton, but the other two disappeared. Two weeks after that, Mr. Brown got influenza, then baby Reg got sick too. We put cold cloths on their fevered heads, made special tea and then put them in the hospital even, but it didn't help. Baby Reg died one day before Mr. Brown.

~

About a month after the funeral, Mrs. Brown looks a little better, like she's in behind her eyes again. We are drinking tea in a patch of spring sunshine that lights up half the kitchen table.

"I went for a walk at dawn today," she says. "I was thinking. I shall be writing to the Home to tell them how much we've loved having you with us." She clears her throat. "As you know, Mr. Brown and I were hoping to move out west this summer, to Calgary. We dreamed of wide open spaces for Reg." She pauses, blinks hard and takes a deep breath. "I've decided to sell the house immediately and go alone."

I am surprised and not surprised. I thought she'd stay for the trial. I thought she would wait to see if the other two men who beat up Mr. Brown would be caught. But Mrs. Brown is a surprising woman. She doesn't even wear a corset.

"Gwen dear, I can't take you with me. I shall have to find employment myself. I have decided that the best thing is to send you back to the Home."

I hold my breath. At the Home they'll look for another family that needs a servant; who knows where I'll end up?

She begins to speak more quickly now, like she's running through her lines in a play. "So I will sell this house. It has too much sorrow in it now. My lawyer has agreed to handle the sale for me and send the money on to the bank in Calgary. And of course I have the savings to tide me over until then. It will be fine. Really." Suddenly she stops talking. Maybe she thinks that the next lines should be mine, but I don't know what they are.

I look at Mrs. Brown's trembling lip and watery eyes. I watch her shaking hand move a teaspoon back and forth across the blue checkered tablecloth, in and out of the sunshine and shadow. And I remember a story called Ruth.

In the Bible there is a story about three women. Naomi has a husband and two sons. The sons have wives, named Orpah and Ruth. One day Naomi's husband dies and then her sons die too. Naomi is *bereft*. That means she's had enough trouble and sorrow. She decides to hike back to her home in Bethlehem. It's a long and dangerous journey, especially for a woman alone. Ruth and Orpah want to go with her. "No, no!" cries Naomi, "Go back to your mothers." Orpah goes. But Ruth says, "Whither thou goest…" which is Bible talk meaning, "If you're going on a dangerous adventure, I'm going with you."

I look at Mrs. Brown's hand and then her eyes. "Don't you remember the Bible story about Ruth?" I ask her. "Don't you remember *whither thou goest?*" One little tear sneaks down Mrs. Brown's cheek. "I can't go back to the Home," I tell her. "You need me."

Mrs. Brown laughs and cries all at once. And then she hugs me for a while and says, "In that case, I suppose I'd best write to the Home and say we are moving to Calgary. And then we'd better start to pack."

The next two weeks are filled with busyness, packing up, cleaning up, and saying goodbye to everyone and everything. I hardly have time to think about anything except shipping crates. I hardly even go to school. When most of the furniture, tools and big things are packed up, sold or given away I begin to say my farewells.

I didn't know it would be so hard to say goodbye to a river, but it was. It was easier to say goodbye to my teacher and the children at school. It was easier to say goodbye to the market and the park with the Joseph Brant statue in it. My friend Molly helped me the whole goodbye time.

"Granny says that you have courage like a bear and that you'll come back here and tell good stories about things out west," Molly tells me. We are standing on the riverbank watching the slow current.

"I wish I could stay, Molly," I say, not looking at her. "I thought this would be my home. I was happy I'd found you and your family. I was happy I'd found the real Canada that Miss Johnson wrote about." Suddenly it feels like a little chunk of ice has got stuck in my throat. I have to wait until it melts before I can talk again.

"But Mrs. Brown can't manage without me. One minute she can't decide whether to pack the tea towels or give them away. She gets up in the middle of the night and walks around the house like a ghost. She forgets to eat. Then suddenly she's all organized, adding up numbers in her bank account and giving orders to the lawyer."

Molly and I stare at the Grand River a while longer. This is the river where Miss Johnson paddled her canoe. I say goodbye to it by reciting her poem, "The Song My Paddle Sings":

West wind, blow from your prairie nest,
Blow from the mountains, blow from the west...

"Write me," Molly says, and puts her arms around me, and I guess our tears eventually make it down into the Grand River and add a little salt to the water.

Back at the house, I open my tin-lined trunk from the Home and place within it three gifts that Molly gave me: sunflower seeds from her mom, "Because you brought sunshine to our house," corn husk dolls which her granny made just for me, and an envelope containing forget-me-not seeds from Molly's own garden. On the front of the envelope, Molly has painted a picture of us together. It's beautiful. Two years ago, I didn't even know I'd be in Canada. Now, I have memories of Canada to pack in my trunk along with my English souvenirs.

I walk through the empty house and stand alone in the sitting room. This had been the heart of the house. Most nights after the dinner dishes were done, Mrs. Brown read out loud, I darned or stitched and Mr. Brown rocked baby Reg to sleep. This is where they made me feel like I belonged in a real family. Sometimes they asked me to recite or to tell stories about my dad, or the Home, or sailing to Canada. I told them about Tim, my best London friend who stowed away on the ship and who plans to be a rich gentleman and buy a theatre where I will perform dazzling plays.

For the last two weeks, the sitting room had been filled with boxes and crates and neighbours helping us sort out the house. We had three piles: Charity, Auction and The West. The neighbour ladies brought food. They also brought a lot of free advice.

"I've held my tongue long enough," Mrs. Weatherby said one day. "I feel I should warn you."

"Warn me about what?" Mrs. Brown asked.

"The wind. I've heard that it never stops howling out there. It can make you lose your mind. And wild cows and bulls race through the Calgary streets! And there are wild Indians. There now. I've said it."

Mrs. Andrews was folding quilts. "What are you talking about? Mohawks live around here; there's no danger!"

"Yes, dear," said Mrs. Black, who believed everything Mrs. Weatherby ever said. "But these are Blackfoot and Cree, not Mohawks. I am sure that they don't write books of poetry like Miss Johnson."

"From what I heard about the Rebellion, I would think that the west is very dangerous," added Mrs. Jones, closing a crate lid with a bang. "I'd never go there."

"But Ida," argued Mrs. Andrews, "the Rebellion wasn't in *Calgary*. And it happened in 1885, thirteen years ago. It's over.

Mrs. Stone stood up and stretched her back. She'd been bent over, packing neatly folded sheets and towels into a crate. "All isn't lost, Christina," she said kindly. "I understand there's a very large opera house, Hull's Opera House. There must be some civility."

Unfortunately, Mrs. Weatherby wasn't finished her warnings. She'd been saving up for her grand finale. "You must keep your wits about you. You too, Gwen. Last summer there was a very dangerous flood in Calgary. You could be swept away! For pity's sake you must immediately learn to swim." Mrs. Brown winked at me and kept on packing. "And most important, you must wear long underwear under your dresses at all times. You can freeze right to death on the prairies."

"There are Chinook winds…" Mrs. Brown began.

"Nonsense!" Mrs. Weatherby continued, "The Reverend George McDougall, Methodist, froze right to death just on the *edge* of Calgary. And *that*," she added firmly, "was only in 1876. There are ferocious blizzards out there, with wind sharp enough to freeze you solid. Not to mention the wolves and coyotes. Mark me, now. Take long underwear. And *never* take it off."

As the ladies were leaving, Mrs. Andrews hung back and put her arm around Mrs. Brown's shoulder. "What I don't understand, Christina, dear," she said, "is why you can't just wait until you have sorted everything out here. You haven't even sold the house yet!"

Mrs. Brown was already nervous about selling the house. She didn't get as much money as she'd thought she would for Mr. Brown's tools, the horse and some of the household items. But everything is in motion now. The date is set, we have the train tickets. The men from the station have already come to collect the furniture and crates to send on ahead. Ready or not, we're on our way.

~

It seems like almost everyone in town comes to the train station to say goodbye. Molly's family drove all the way in from the Reserve, too. It is wonderful, sad and exciting, all mixed together.

To get to the west from Brantford, we first travel east to Toronto and change trains. We settle in our seats and watch the farmland and Lake Ontario drift past our window. Mrs. Brown's jaw is set tight and her eyes seem far away, so I sit near her and keep quiet.

In Toronto, we board the train for Calgary. It is more elaborate than the first train. These seats are upholstered in rich green cloth. The walls are shiny wood and fancy gas lamps hang from the ceiling. Our porter is Joseph, a Black man with sparkly eyes. "I'll be lookin' after you both," he says. "Anything you want, you tell me." He tells us we will arrive in Calgary before dawn on Monday, three full days and a bit.

"Thank you, Joseph," Mrs. Brown says. Before he even leaves the car, she puts her head against the back of the seat and falls fast asleep.

I cannot leave her to explore the train; I must watch over her. So I take *White Wampum* out of my bag and hold the brown-red book gently between my hands. I remember the night I watched Miss Johnson from the shadows backstage. She *dazzled* that audience with her poems about Canada.

I open the book to "Pilot of the Plains" because that's where we are going, to the plains. In this poem, a white man and an Indian woman named Yakonwita are in love. The white man goes away. People tell the woman to forget him, but she won't. In summer, *she scans the rolling prairie where the foothills fall, and rise* and waits.

And then winter comes to *the pathless prairie*. This is the part where the paleface calls, *Yakonwita, I am coming love, at last.* But on his way back to her, he gets *lost and benumbed* and as he sinks into the snowdrifts, he calls her name again. Faraway, Yakonwita leaves her tepee and searches for him. But then she gets lost and benumbed, too. And the end of the story is:

Late at night, say Indian hunters, when the starlight clouds
    or wanes,
Far away they see a maiden, misty as the autumn rains,
Guiding with her lamp of moonlight
Hunters lost upon the plains.

Maybe Mrs. Weatherby read that poem and that's why she thinks we need long underwear in Calgary all year long. We'll soon find out, I suppose.

I look out the train window at Ontario's farms and trees and lakes, and wonder how it will be to live on the plains. I hope I get to see the *lamp of moonlight,* but I sincerely hope I never get lost like the pale-faced lover or the Reverend George McDougall, Methodist, and get benumbed and die. I start conjuring up a play called, "London Girl Sweeps Across the Plains and Bedazzles the Crowds at the Calgary Opera House," but the swaying of the train makes me sleepy. I doze off thinking that maybe Mrs. Brown will be alright if I can just pilot her across the plains to Calgary.

~

I wake up suddenly because I feel someone staring at me. He is standing in the aisle, and his dark eyes seem to drill holes in my head. He blinks and stares at Mrs. Brown with the same intensity. He is tall, with brown hair and a brown handlebar moustache. He wears a dark gray suit and green vest with a thick gold watch chain looped across his little pot belly. When I meet his gaze, he turns suddenly and walks away, into the next car. I wonder, have I seen him before?

Pilot

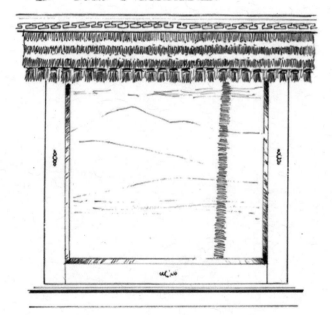

Joseph sees me reading *White Wampum*. "Oh," he says, "are you acquainted with the lady poet?"

I can tell this is a trick question, so I turn it back to him, "No. Are you?"

He smiles broadly. "Yes! She travels often across this country. Sometimes I'm lucky enough to be her porter. She is a gracious lady."

I am thrilled that he knows her, but before I can pepper him with questions, he sends us to the dining room where we eat like queens. We have a splendid meal of salmon, potatoes and peas which I have not had to cook, and it is served on plates which I do not have to wash. It is luxury. I feel like a lady and I try to eat like one, with dainty bites and holding my silverware just so. It is a funny thing to eat in a swaying train. The water in our glasses moves gently to and fro.

When we leave the dining car, the floor sways beneath our feet as we walk down the aisles. When the train rounds a corner, I hold the backs of the seats to keep steady. It reminds me of walking my old dad home from the pub. The ground wasn't swaying, but he was, and I'd have to hold him upright to get him all the way home and up the stairs to our little flat in London.

We walk through four cars to get back to our own. Joseph has magically turned our seats into berths and made our beds. Before we reach the town of North Bay, Ontario, the train rocks me to sleep.

I dream about a river. Not the Thames in London or the Grand in Brantford. This is a fast, strong river near the Rocky Mountains. I am in a canoe, but the paddles are in the river. I can see them on the left, just ahead, out of reach. The wind is strong, pushing my dress like a sail. Faster and faster the canoe hurtles past the rocks and the open places, the willows, the duck nests. Past the poplars, a fox den, past a big pile of white bones. I stand up and see the pathless prairie ahead. I cannot steer the canoe or get to shore.

Suddenly I hear a roar. A great brown bear on the bank is holding a long brown rope. *"Hiya!"* the bear calls. "Hold on, girl!" She throws me the rope and gently pulls me to shore. I wake up thinking about her and other bears I have learned about since I came to Canada. Here I learned about *Ursa Major* in the night sky. That was when I first arrived and met a lumberjack on the train from Quebec City to Toronto.

His name was Pierre Paul. I asked if he ever got lost in the woods and he said, "You never get lost when you look up and see dat ol' bear. She will guide you, *yessir!"* And he was right because when I had to hike through the Ontario bush by myself, I felt a great comfort knowing that she was up there, guiding me.

And then I think about the bear I saw in the forest eating raspberries and how she didn't hurt me. I remember Molly and her granny's magical Mohawk story about the great bear and the three hunters that ended up turning the maple leaves red and then flying up to become star people. I hope I meet kind people like Pierre Paul, Molly and Gran in Calgary. I hope Mrs. Weatherby is wrong about wild cows and freezing to death and all that.

In the morning, Joseph announces that we've stopped in Chapleau, Ontario, to hook on a new dining car. I peek through the curtains that hang around my berth and see a girl my age doing a little dance down the aisle on the way to the toilet. Strands of curly red hair have escaped from the bun at the back of her head. She wears a plain, grey wool dress that goes down to the top of her black boot tops and a happy smile on her freckled face.

I scramble into my blue wool dress, hoping to meet her in the dining car. Mrs. Brown is already there, drinking coffee and looking out at the forest. When she sees me, the girl jumps up. "I so hope you are going to the Northwest Territories like us," she says, without even being introduced. "Travelling with all old people is a humbling experience and I was wishing for a companion my own age. How old are you?" That's how Janey talks, with words like *humbling*.

The waiter asks her to sit down and she takes a seat at our table and keeps talking. "I've sailed all the way from Scotland, have been on the train for four days, and to be honest, it's getting boring. I saw you get on yesterday, but you seemed busy with your mother. My mother *forbade* me to bother you. I was glad when it was morning and I was *liberated* from her rule. My name is Janey Williamson."

While Mrs. Brown finishes her coffee and I eat porridge, Janey tells us that her uncle has a ranch in the foothills, whatever that is, near Calgary. "My uncle thinks my da will make a good rancher, but my *long-suffering* mother and I don't. He cannot *restore or repair* anything and always bangs his thumb with a hammer. He's never ridden on a horse and knows nothing about cows. But," she says optimistically, "he's got the spunk. So I figure he'll make something out of it. It's an adventure."

The thing about Janey is that she makes your heart glad and she even makes Mrs. Brown laugh out loud. Janey doesn't know about all the tragedy in our life, so she doesn't know to be careful about how she talks. This is a very good thing because sometimes when people do know, they tiptoe around tragedies, and often what sad people really need is a good laugh.

We laugh a lot while we travel on and on and *on* in the province of Ontario, toward the *pathless prairie*. For one thing, we laugh trying to teach English to Olga.

Olga's family is in the next car and they smell like something different and speak another language, not even French. Mrs. Brown thinks it's Russian. Olga is our age and has brown braids pinned on top of her head. We found her on the first day after breakfast. We invite her to be our friend using sign language, and her mother nods and says, "*da, da*" and "*spaseebo,*" which means, "Go ahead and have some fun," I think.

We all laugh a lot trying to avoid the demon, Mr. Greene. Mr. Greene swooped down on us when Olga, Janey and I were eating our first lunch together. He is a teacher from what he calls *The Olde Country,* which is England, and he's very excited to find three girls to practise teaching on. He hopes to find a teaching position in Victoria, that's a city named after our gracious queen and it's on Vancouver Island in British Columbia. Mr. Greene told us that. He has studied a lot about Canada, and wants to tell us everything he knows. *Everything.*

"Come to the next car and I shall begin your instruction. You must not enter the west *ignorant,*" he tells us. I look to Mrs. Brown for help, but she merely shrugs and smiles, which I think means, *Why not?* Mrs. Williamson just laughs. Olga's mama bobs her head in imitation of the other ladies, so Mr. Greene knows we are trapped. If we don't appear after breakfast and lunch for our lesson, he walks through the cars, searching for us. As the forests give way to even more forests, our days give way to a rhythm.

Mr. Greene's first lesson is *Important Facts about the Golden West.* "Calgary is the principal city on the railway in the district of Alberta in the Northwest Territories," he says. "It's in the centre of the cattle district. There are many modern amenities in the town, such as electrical lights. The population is around four thousand. There are people from Europe, the British Isles and some from China who arrived in Canada to build the railway. You will also see Blackfoot people, and some from the Cree nation. We are likely to see some teepees along the way as we get closer."

When he notices some adults listening, he becomes self conscious. "Oh, I do wish I had some slates with me," he complains to no one in particular. As if writing on slate with chalk would make his lesson more interesting. He blushes when he sees two ladies smiling at him. We tell him later that they are Miss Cookson and Miss Montgomery, and they are going to work as Victorian nurses in Medicine Hat. He blushes even more. Victorian nurses are nurses named for our gracious queen in England. They are special, I guess.

But Mr. Greene does know a lot about the West, and that is good, it's just that his lessons go on and on, like the province of Ontario. Poor Olga doesn't understand English, but with his steely gaze he seems to have the power to make her sit there.

At dinner, I see that the man with the brown, handlebar moustache is sitting a few tables down from us. Opposite him is a younger man drinking a glass of water. He is missing the baby finger on his right hand. Suddenly, the older man laughs and I see that he has a gold tooth. It is hard not to stare.

"Do you know those men?" I ask Mrs. Brown.

She studies them, holding the menu up to her face so it's not obvious. "Vaguely familiar," she says. "They're Brantford men, but I don't know their names." She doesn't seem very interested.

Dinner arrives, and Mrs. Brown begins her meal. But I keep watching the men in the reflection of the window. Suddenly, Gold Tooth looks up. Our eyes meet. His eyes are hard and mean. I look away.

The next morning, Olga, Janey and I decide to tour the train from one end to the other. Just as we are leaving the second car, we see Mr. Greene coming down the aisle. "Quick!" Janey says, "get down!" and trying to smother our giggles, we squat behind the end seats and hope Mr. Greene will not look down as he passes. Then I realize that we are just behind the Brantford men.

"I'm sure she hasn't recognized us, Frank," says Gold Tooth. "And anyway, she can't pin anything on us, or connect us in any way. We're just Brantford business men, moving to Calgary. Nothing so unusual about that."

"You're right, Charlie. You're always right," says Missing Finger. "I don't know about the kid, though."

"She did give me a look, but c'mon. Even if she did figure it out, who'd believe an orphan from the Home? She's just a brat. Forget it."

I am so caught up in listening that I almost scream when Mr. Greene's face appears above us. "There you are!" he says happily. "Found you! Don't you realize it's time for your lesson? Come along, we have a lot of things to learn." I follow along, but I am wondering, "Orphan? What are they talking about? Who are these men and why do they look so nasty?" But soon I am learning about buffalo.

"The buffalo, or *bison,* stand about five or six feet high at the shoulder. They can weigh between one thousand and two thousand pounds. They live on the open plain," he begins. An old man stops to listen. He leans on the back of a seat while Mr.

Greene drones on about buffalo habitat. His name, we soon learn, is Jack Temple.

While Mr. Greene wears a dapper suit cut in the latest English fashion with a big, white, starched collar and a polka dot bow tie, Jack Temple's clothes are the opposite. He wears rumpled pants and a shirt with no tie. His fringed leather boots are old. He wears a dark leather vest with Indian beadwork, and a stained felt hat that he never takes off. Side by side, these men make a stunning looking pair.

"I remember the buffalo days," Jack says quietly, "great, thundering herds of wild ones all around. This was in the days when I first come west by ox and cart, long before this here railway. Them herds was a sight." Mr. Greene stops talking and sits down with us and listens. "Now there's naught but a few sprinklings of cows comin' up from the States. Stupid weak things, cattle are, dyin' by the dozens in winter blizzards; not tough like the buffalo.

"Buffalo was king of the prairie in them days. People used up every bit of the buffaloes they killed, too. Hides were turned into blankets, clothes, ropes and teepees. They 'et the meat. Bones and horns were made into tools. Sinews were made into strong thread. No wonder the people spoke to the spirit of the buffalo and thanked it for its life."

Jack sighs and looks out the window with watery eyes. "'Tis all changed now. The railway done it, bringing in settlers wanting farms and ranches. White fellas from the east stickin' their rifles out the train windows and just shootin' at the herds. Didn't pay no never mind to nothin'. Never 'et 'em or used 'em for anything. Killed 'em for fun, they did. Some went out later, gathered up the bones and shipped 'em east. Made bone meal fertilizer with the skeletons."

I look at Janey; her eyes are big as saucers. Olga may not understand all the words, but she looks as amazed as I feel. I'm picturing huge skeletons of buffaloes wandering across the pathless prairie, looking for home. Looking for their families. Looking for themselves. Mr. Greene says nothing. He's on the edge of his seat too.

"Got so downhearted, I moved east again," Jack Temple says. "But the people I knew out there is all dead, so I'm headin' back west. Might go the way of the buffalo myself. Just disappear. No place for me now, neither."

No one says anything for a long, sad time, not even Mr. Greene. Jack turns and walks back to his own car.

It is hard to shake off the sadness of Jack Temple's lesson, but at dinner Olga, Janey and I sit opposite the Flower Sisters, and that helps. Their real names are Pansy and Violet, and they are going all the way to the gold fields in the Yukon. They are corset ladies so they're squeezed in the middle and fluffed out at both ends. They have fancy feathers on their hats and lace around their necklines.

"We sing—" says Miss Pansy.

"—we dance," finishes Miss Violet.

"There's a lot of lonely men in the northwest we heard—" Miss Pansy says giggling.

"—so we plan to entertain them," adds her sister.

I would like to have asked them more about the entertainment business, but just then Mr. Greene comes down the aisle, looking for us. He is determined to teach us about the building of the Canadian Pacific Railway and needs to catch up on the lessons he's planned, since Jack Temple took over some of his teaching time this afternoon. We agree to a second lesson after dinner.

By this time, Janey's mother and Mrs. Brown have become friends. Olga's mother sits near them, knitting. She seems glad to be in the company of other women, even if they can't really talk. Piloting Mrs. Brown across the plains isn't so hard after all.

Olga, Janey and I walk down the gently swaying car to hear about William van Horne, Chief Crowfoot and Father Lacombe. But talking to the Flower Sisters has given me an idea, and it's hard to concentrate on Mr. Greene's story about Prime Minister Sir John A. Macdonald's plans to unite Canada from sea to shining sea, because I'm planning something great.

Even Mr. Greene thinks my idea is a good one when I tell him about it after the lesson. We are going to hold a concert. Anyone can be in it. Mr. Greene will make a list of performers. I have already decided to let him be the master of ceremonies.

As we are leaving Manitoba, we pass the word about the concert so that people have all of Saskatchewan to think about what they want to do. I am too busy to think about Missing Finger and Gold Tooth, and I do not see them again. I think they probably got off the train in Winnipeg.

~

Sunday night just east of the town of Medicine Hat, the concert begins. Olga's father plays accordion while she and her mother sing a ballad. I can hear the loneliness in her father's music, even though I don't understand the Russian words.

Janey and her mother sing, "My Bonnie Lies Over the Ocean." I'm surprised how much the song reminds me of my old dad. Sometimes when I'd go along to the pub to bring him home, he'd sing songs like that at the top of his voice.

Jack Temple plays "Buffalo Days" on his harmonica. I go last. "The Cattle Thief" is by Pauline Johnson and I recite it by heart. It begins,

They were coming across the prairie, they were galloping hard and fast;
For the eyes of those desperate riders had sighted their man at last…

It is the story of Eagle Chief. The buffalo are all gone and his family was starving, so he killed a cow. The settlers tracked him down and shot him with *a dozen balls of lead*. Then they were going to chop him up and feed his body to the wolves but

> *...the first stroke was arrested by a woman's strange, wild cry;*
> *And out into the open, with a courage past belief,*
> *She dashed and spread her blanket o'er the corpse of the*
> *   Cattle Thief;*
> *And the words outleapt from her shrunken lips in the language*
> *   of the Cree,*
> *"If you mean to touch that body, you must cut your way*
> *   through me."*
> *And that band of cursing settlers dropped backward one by*
> *   one,*
> *For they knew that an Indian woman roused, was a woman*
> *   to let alone.*

The poem ends when she says:

> *Give back our land and our country, give back our herds of*
> *   game;*
> *Give back the furs and the forests that were ours before you*
> *   came;*
> *Give back the peace and the plenty. Then come with your*
> *   new belief;*
> *And blame, if you dare, the hunger that drove him to be a*
> *   thief.*

When I finish, people don't say a word or move. The train chugs toward the setting sun, the only sound is of wheels on steel. Then one person begins to clap. It is Jack Temple. "Good girl. Bravo!" he says, and slowly, the others join in. Mrs. Brown has tears in her eyes; that's the sign of a good performance.

Olga's family leaves the train in Medicine Hat. Even though we don't speak the same language, our hugs are the same in English and Russian.

~

An almost-full moon watches our small, drowsy group get off the train in Calgary. Our footsteps echo loud on the wooden sidewalk as we make our way slowly through the dark, sleeping town to the hotel on Stephen Avenue. I see that Gold Tooth and Missing Finger are still with us after all. They walk quickly ahead of the Williamsons, Mrs. Brown and I. Jack Temple follows behind us. Goosebumps rise on the back of my neck when coyotes howl in the distance.

Arrival

"Howdy," says the waitress. " Welcome to the Sandstone City. I'm Irene." She sets huge plates of scrambled eggs, toast, jam, fried potatoes, bacon and beefsteak down on the blue-checkered tablecloth in front of Janey and me. "Think that's enough to hold you 'til lunch?" I've never seen that much food on one plate; Mrs. Williamson and Mrs. Brown laugh quietly.

"I hope all you ladies will like it here. If you don't mind long hours and hard work, you'll go far in Calgary. They say that this town is going to boom." She fills the coffee cups with dark fragrant coffee. "It's true we're in a bit of a Depression now, but Calgary's motto is 'Onward.' I believe it. And, if you're in the market for a man, there are plenty to choose from. For every one of us there are two of them!" She wipes her hands on her apron and heads back to the kitchen laughing.

Mrs. Brown laughs too, a good sound. "I wonder if all westerners are so optimistic," she says, carefully spreading butter on a thick slab of toast. "I like it here already."

Everyone who got off the train last night is here in the hotel dining room except Jack Temple. I ask Irene if she knows him.

"Everyone knows Jack, even though he doesn't talk much. I figured he wouldn't last long out east—too wild for Toronto now. He likely headed for the hills at dawn." She nods slightly in the direction of Gold Tooth and Missing Finger and lowers her voice. "Say, know anything about those shifty-eyed gentlemen? They came in with you, didn't they?" I look across the dining room. Their eyes are on their breakfasts.

"Those gentlemen didn't make conversation," Mrs. Williamson says, "They kept to themselves on the train."

"I've seen them in Brantford," Mrs. Brown says slowly. She seems to be thinking about something else.

A woman and a boy about my age enter the dining room. Mrs. McBride surveys the room then marches straight to our table. She introduces herself and Melvin. "Will you be staying in Calgary?" she asks. Without waiting for an answer, she continues. "This hotel suits us. We live here," she says proudly, "Melvin and I think it's lovely. My husband is out of town often. *On business*," she stresses. Melvin has cold, hard eyes.

"Is this a school holiday?" I ask him.

"Melvin has a bad cold. I've kept him with me today," his mother answers.

The door opens again and a man wearing a cowboy hat pulled down over red hair bursts into the room. "Where're my Scottish lassies?" he bellows.

"Mercy!" says Mrs. McBride, pulling Melvin out of the way.

Janey leaps up from the table and runs into his arms. "You can't mean that this beauty is the wee bairn I left behind in Scotland?" he roars, lifting her off her feet and swinging her around.

Mrs. Brown and I watch the family reunion change the air in

the dining room from plain to joyous in an instant. The door opens again, and a cowboy and a boy about our age enter quietly. He shakes Janey's hand formally. "I'm your cousin Wilbur," he says.

The three pull chairs up to our table and Irene is soon pouring coffee and bringing out more mountains of food. Janey's uncle tells us his ranch is in Cochrane, only two hours away. He promises he'll bring her into town sometimes "as long as she's chopped the wood, fed the chickens, baked the pies, mended the fences and helped with the branding." Janey looks at me, turns red, then laughs helplessly.

"Aw, Dad," Wilbur says, "don't tease her right away."

All too soon, breakfast is over. The Williamsons have loaded their luggage onto the buckboard, and we are standing on the wooden sidewalk in bright April sunshine. I swallow the lump in my throat and we wave them out of sight, as they head toward the mountains. I hold tight to the piece of paper with Janey's address on it. At least we can write.

When they are only a speck in the distance, Mrs. Brown and I decide to tour Calgary. The sky is a bright blue canopy over us; the air feels sparkly and crisp. The town is awake and busy.

We walk slowly, taking in our new home. The buildings are different from Brantford and Toronto and London. Some are made of wood, but many on Stephen Avenue are sandstone; we see why

Calgary is called "The Sandstone City." This town is brand new and looks like it's ready for an adventure, like us.

We walk the length of the main street, among cowboys wearing Stetsons and jingly spurs, Blackfoot people wearing blanket coats and silver jewelry, gentlemen in worsted suits and bowler hats, and ladies wearing fancy or plain cotton dresses. Modern carriages, horses with fancy saddles or simple blankets, pony carts and bicycles all share the wide main street.

Suddenly Mrs. Brown stops in her tracks. She steps into the middle of the street and turns in a circle. "Even though I knew that the Prairie was bald, I couldn't really imagine what that would *feel* like," she says. "There are hardly any trees here. We must plant trees!"

There's everything for sale on Stephen Avenue! Tobacco, watches, shoes, music, groceries, harnesses, timber, sewing machines and hardware—why, you can even get embalmed! The big Hudson's Bay store looks like it has just about everything. Mrs. Brown peers into the photographer's shop window. "I think we ought to have our photograph taken," she says smiling. "We could send it back to Brantford to prove we haven't been eaten by bears, frozen to death or trampled by cows yet!" At the mention of cows, I look around sharp in every direction. But except for some grazing far in the distance, I don't see any danger.

But there's more to see: a bakery, police station, insurance and dental offices, and law firms. I can't imagine lacking for anything here. Why, we could even order a telephone at the Bell Telephone

Exchange! It seems funny to find the name of the Brantford inventor all the way out here.

On the porch of the general store, there is a lady wrapped in a white wool blanket with red, green and yellow stripes on it. She sits quietly watching the street. She has sparkly eyes, a brown face with wrinkles and long braids. I smile at her and she winks back. She makes me think of a mountain. Suddenly three big boys come out from the store. "Old squaw!" sneers the tallest, "get out of the way."

"Somebody ought to get rid of people like her," says his friend, a sharp-faced boy wearing a tweed cap. A boy with spectacles laughs and they run down the street.

Inside, Mrs. Brown asks the proprietor about her. "Is the lady outside begging?"

"Nope. Just watching the town. Keeping an eye on things. She doesn't hurt anyone. I tried to get her to leave, but she just comes back. She's too big to lift or push, and since she doesn't bother anyone, I just accept the fact that she's part of the town. She was here when I bought the store and I guess she'll be here when I sell it and leave."

"Those boys were rude to her," Mrs. Brown says.

"They're just kids," the proprietor answers. "Boys will be boys!" he smiles, but Mrs. Brown doesn't smile. "People call her 'Grand Mary.'"

I roll the words around in my head as I feel in my pocket for a penny to pay for a peppermint candy, "Grand Mary, Grand Mary." I wonder what stories she knows. I think about Molly's grandma on the Reserve and feel a sharp pang of loneliness.

"Yep," says the proprietor, "Grand Mary is part of the Calgary landscape. She and Big Tom live on the other side of the river where it's wilderness. If you go over the bridge, turn right, and follow a footpath, you'll come to their camp. I stumbled on it when I was looking for a good spot to fish. It's not far out of town." I am all ears, but there is no time for that now. Mrs. Brown is leaving; there's more town to explore.

The street runs east and west; we stand still a moment just to look. There are some houses toward the east, beyond the curve of the Elbow River, but then the wide open prairie goes on and on forever. Well, not forever, but back to Regina, Winnipeg, all the way to Ontario.

Beyond the western edge of town, distant teepees dot the hills; far beyond them somewhere is the Williamson Ranch, and farther still are the Rocky Mountains. They are blue and white and seem very close, even though I know they are eighty miles away. Mrs. Brown says one day we'll take the train out to visit the fancy hotel and hot springs in Banff.

People smile as they pass us; it seems friendly here. We look in all the shop windows. Then we walk nine blocks north to the Bow River, rushing cold and clear from the Rockies. There are bushes and poplar trees along the river bank. We meet magpies, bigger than crows. They are black and white with long, long tails—sassy birds that laugh and call to us as we pass. In the mud, we see deer tracks and near the bridge, a beaver lodge. Looping back toward the main part of town we have lunch in a tea room, then Mrs. Brown says she's had enough. "I need a nap, but you are free to explore for one hour. Not a minute longer, please."

I ask our waitress for directions. She points out the window and draws a map in the air. "Hull's Opera House is near Knox Presbyterian Church. You can't miss it."

It looks almost like a church itself, with the doors and windows topped by round, arched windows. Three circle windows have crosses inside and there are four cupolas on the roof.

I am standing by the side door, when suddenly it bursts open and a cloud of dust and dirt sweep out onto the road. A man holding a broom pops his head out at my little squeal of surprise. He is as startled to see me as I am to see him.

"Hey!" he says, "why aren't you in school?" He is old, with more hair in his ears, eyebrows and under his nose than on his head. His grey moustache is droopy like a walrus's. He wears a rumpled brown shirt, red suspenders to hold up his patched trousers and scuffed cowboy boots with rundown heels.

"It's my first day in Calgary," I say, "I'm just looking around."

He bows with a dramatic flourish. "Well then, welcome, young lady! My name's Willie."

"My dad used to be a cleaner in a theatre in London, England," I tell him.

"You'd best have a look inside, then," he says, "and see how Calgary measures up to grand old London. We're pretty proud of this place. It seats a thousand—it's the best opera house between Winnipeg and Vancouver. We even have our own Calgary Operatic Society. Last year they put on *Pirates of Penzance* by Mr. Gilbert and Mr. Sullivan. We're just like the big cities now!"

Three splendid chandeliers hang from the ceiling and there are three tiers of seats on the balcony. "Go on," Willie says, "go up the steps and stand on the stage. See how that feels."

It's the smell that makes me feel like crying. I feel happy and sad at the same time. The smell is of wood and hot footlights and sweat and grease paint and beautiful people. It reminds me of watching Miss Pauline Johnson with my dad.

He had sneaked me backstage so I had to be very still and small to watch. Miss Pauline Johnson is the most beautiful lady I've ever seen. She knows how to makes words dance in the air. The audience went wild when she finished her performance. They loved her and so did I. One day I will write story poems and plays, and I'll stand on the stage with silk and feathers and satin shoes, too.

I look down at my boots and see they have mud on them, but I walk up the steps to the centre of the stage and look out at the sea of empty chairs.

"Come on, then," says Willie. He leans his broom against the wall and takes a seat with a plop. "Let's have a song. Or could you recite?"

I bow to the old man and close my eyes for a minute. I take a deep breath and announce the poem from White Wampum. "'Dawendine.' A poem by Miss Pauline Johnson."

There's a spirit on the river, there's a ghost upon the shore,
They are chanting, they are singing through the starlight
      evermore,
As they steal amid the silence
And the shadows of the shore.
You can hear them when the Northern candles light the
      Northern sky,
Those pale, uncertain candle flames, that shiver, dart and die,
Those dead man's icy finger tips,
Athwart the Northern sky...

Willie sits up straight in his seat and I recite the story of the *ringing war-cry of a long-forgotten brave* and Dawendine's *singing spirit*. It is the story about a woman whose brother is killed. To save the rest of her people, Dawendine has to take the white wampum belt to make peace with the killer. All by herself she has to do it. The poem calls her *the dawn of peace.*

Even though I've read that poem a million times, it makes the hairs on my arms stand up when I say it out loud in that great big empty theatre, with old Willie sitting on the edge of his seat, not even blinking. When I'm finished, Willie jumps to his feet and gives me a standing ovation.

I'm just thinking that the next play I'll write will be, "London Home Child Travels to Calgary and Performs in the Wild West" but then, like a gunshot, the front door bursts open. Two cowboys rush in. "Willie, there's been another killing. You better saddle up." The men don't say anything to me or even see me standing alone on the stage. They turn and rush out, banging the door behind them.

"What happened?" I ask. "Who's been killed?"

"There's been two cattle killed on Nose Hill in the past two weeks," he says. "We don't know who done it, but we'll find them. I got to lock up this place. You done a good recitation, young lady. I'll see you back here at a real performance some time."

Out on the street I see six cowboys on horseback waiting for Willie. They are all carrying guns.

I race all the way back to the hotel. I cannot believe that real cowboys with real guns ride down the streets of Calgary. Who needs to make up stories about this place? No one will even believe the truth! I cannot wait to tell Mrs. Brown about the murdered cow, but when I get there, she is in no mood to hear about cows. She's sitting on the edge of the bed. I can tell that she's been crying. A telegram lies on her lap.

"What happened?" I ask.

"Money," she says. "The telegram is from the realtor. The house in Brantford didn't sell after all; the deal fell through. He warned that buyers are few and far between right now, so we shouldn't count on selling anytime soon. I don't know what we will do when my savings run out." She heaves a deep, deep sigh.

Mrs. Brown looks exhausted and sad. I guess I do have to keep piloting her. Maybe I need to find work here as a servant. There are some very fancy houses in Calgary, so there are likely lots of jobs for servants.

Suddenly, she stands and walks to the window with short, quick steps. "We need to get out of this hotel and find a house to rent. We need to be able to cook our own meals instead of paying in restaurants. And I need to find work and make some money."

River House

The next morning, Mrs. Brown seems stronger. We have an early breakfast in the dining room. Melvin stares at me but doesn't say anything.

"And how are you getting on?" Mrs. McBride asks. Without waiting for an answer, she lowers her voice and says, "Terrible about the cattle rustlers, isn't it? Lawless place, that's what. I'm sure that if my husband was a policeman, he'd be able to find out who's doing it. Terrible to take another person's property, I say. Dishonest people should be hung."

Mrs. Brown smiles to show she's listening, but doesn't say anything to all that. She takes a sip of coffee and then says, "We are looking for a house today. Would you know of one for rent? It needs to be inexpensive. And perhaps you know of some office employment available?"

Melvin's mother shakes her head and frowns. She looks disappointed, as if she was hoping we'd be shocked about the cattle rustlers.

"And Melvin?" continues Mrs. Brown. "How are you feeling today? Perhaps you might walk Gwen to school when we're settled? Perhaps you could introduce her to your friends?"

"Depends on his bad cold," Mrs. McBride says. "We'll see."

I would rather walk to school with a bleedin' rattlesnake than with Melvin, but I don't want to say that to Mrs. Brown. She was only trying to be kind.

At the newspaper office we buy a *Herald* newspaper and spread it out right on the counter. We see advertisements for general servants, cooks, farm implements, cattle and Eau Claire milled lumber. Then we find a listing that says, *House for Rent on Bow River, north side. Ten dollars monthly. Needs some work. Apply Mr. Smith. Clarence Block, Stephen Avenue.*

"We can afford ten dollars," she says. "Let's get the key and take a look."

It's a sunny day. We walk along Stephen Avenue then turn north. Our shadows are long. When we get close to the river, we see dozens of little brown gophers. They stand up on two legs and watch our progress with sharp black eyes. They whistle to one another and pop in and out of their holes like lightning.

We cross the bridge. If we stay on the road, it will lead us all the way to Edmonton. There are a few houses nearby, but we leave the road and turn left onto a wheel-rutted track that runs alongside the river. We are only about fifteen minutes from the hotel, but it's very different on this side of the river, just a few ranch houses dotted around. There are still leftover flood memories from last year—some roots from upturned trees reach for the sky. Long grasses and sticks are still caught in the willows. But it is pretty here, and I like the sound of the river and the smell of the rich soil. Overhead, a vee of Canada geese circles around. Mrs. Brown has walked on ahead of me and I must run to catch up.

Then, suddenly, there it is, a wooden house standing lonely up from the bank; a hill rising behind it. It's like the house is on stage and the cliff is a back drop. Around it, poplars are misted with green buds ready to burst into spring. There is an outhouse and clothesline behind the house and a water pump in the front. Last year's swallows' nest clings to the eaves, but there's no bird near it now.

Mrs. Brown opens the door with the black iron key and steps inside. "Oh my," she says. "Oh no." And then she wilts, as if all the air has been let out of her. She slides down along the door frame to the floor, her eyes big. Little dust beams fly up in the sunshine and dance in the air over her head. No one but the wind, insects and small animals have lived here for a while, it seems. I try to think of something encouraging to say, but as I look around carefully, I see there's not much to be encouraged about.

"Never mind, Mrs. Brown, what do you think they trained me for in London? I'll have this house cleaned up in no time, and then the men will bring along the furniture and our trunks from the storage at the railway. We'll be fine, really we will," I say, trying to sound convincing and brave.

The house is a mess. Dirt, animal droppings and bits of grass and twigs are everywhere. The windows are streaked with dirt, and one in the sitting room is broken. The kitchen smells musty where there are piles of newspapers and garbage near the wood stove. Long minutes pass. Finally, Mrs. Brown slides up the door frame again and walks through the house. There are two bedrooms upstairs. On the main floor are a large storeroom, sitting room and kitchen. A mouse has nested in the oven of the wood stove.

We march back to town, pay ten dollars to Mr. Smith, then buy a wheelbarrow at the general store to carry the hammer, nails, broom, soap, vinegar, washing soda, rags, pails and mops we need to turn that house into our home. Grand Mary is sitting on the porch again. I smile and tell her my name. She nods and continues to survey the street in silence.

Side by side, Mrs. Brown and I work hard all afternoon. We carry out garbage brought in by the wind and mice. We shake the stovepipes and carry the soot to the outhouse. We pump water from the well and carry it into the house to scrub and polish.

The windows soon sparkle. We carry our pails of vinegar and water outside to empty them. We are sweating. "Take a break, dear," Mrs. Brown says, wiping her face on her apron. I don't need two invitations to run down the bank to the river. I've been dying to poke around down there all day.

I walk through the willows and stand on the stony shore. Across the river, the town looks cosy in the sunshine. I see the church spires, the hospital, the top of Hull's Opera House. The streets, already busy, are neatly laid out in a pattern. West along the river, just before the lumber mill, a small herd of cattle grazes. I walk in the opposite direction. and remember walking with Molly along the Grand River. This river, like the Grand, is bursting with life. Magpies call each other from the poplars. Overhead, ravens play in the wind. Mallard ducks swim along the shore, looking for good nesting places. Then, I catch a different movement out of the corner of my eye. Molly always said if you want to see the animals, you must become as still as a stone. I wait.

All at once I hear a yip from the river bank ahead. Still, I don't move. Suddenly a red fox walks into view. She has a white tip on her bushy tail. Her feet and ear tips are black. A limp brown rabbit dangles from her jaws. I hold my breath.

Hesitating only a moment, she dashes across the open space and disappears into a hole in the bank behind the small willow bushes. I tiptoe closer. Right above the den, another fox is watching me. He yaps and trots along a path in clear view. He stops and turns to see what I am doing. I climb the bank and follow through the trees, just like he wants me to. Within seconds, the fox has disappeared, but I am sure he is watching me as I walk.

Ahead of me, a movement, like a shadow, makes me stop. Again I stand still and wait. A big woman, wrapped in a white blanket with red, green and black stripes, steps across the path. It's Grand Mary. I raise my hand to wave, but in an instant she has vanished from sight. I listen. The river gurgles, the trees sigh in the breeze, magpies call in the distance, and that is all. I remember Mrs. Brown; she might be worried. I turn and quickly retrace my steps back to the house.

Mrs. Brown is looking for me, shielding her eyes from the late afternoon sun. "I was afraid you got lost, dear," she says, a little half smile on her lips.

Before the sun sets, we've banished the cobwebs, shined the windows and swept the floors. We are finished for this day. Before we leave, I carry the mouse nest outside and place it in the bushes beyond the house. That's when I see the man down by the river. His back is to me. I stand and watch as he gently pulls his fishing pole this way and that, slowly, slowly, then raises his arm again and casts his hook far out into the green running water. It is graceful, like a slow, beautiful dance.

I walk down the bank a little to see better. He has one long braid down his back. He's wearing a little black shiny hat with no brim. His shoes are like black slippers, rather worn. He pretends he cannot see me coming, but I know he can; I'm in plain view. I stand on the bank and he stands down on the stony shore. Three dead fish lie at his feet.

"Hello?" I call.

He turns around slowly. "Ho!" he says, and then looks over my head and up and down the bank. He looks nervous.

"Nice fish you have!" I say.

The man looks around again, pulls his line out of the water, twirls it around his pole. He picks up his three fish, all strung together with twine through their gills.

I wish he would stay so I can watch him fish, but he climbs the bank and starts walking away. Suddenly he stops. "You like fish?" Before I answer, he takes one fish off his string, lays it near my feet, bows, then walks away with short, quick steps.

"You are so stupid," says a voice. I whirl around and recognize Melvin's jeering face as it suddenly appears from behind the willow bushes in front of me.

"What's wrong with you?" I ask, pretending he didn't scare me half to death. "Why are you spying on me?"

"I like to know what's going on. I like to know things, like you're going to live in that rickety old house that's probably going to fall apart any minute. Anyway, everybody knows about this fishing spot. I see kids fishing here all the time. Big fancy lawyers from town come, too. Sometimes one of the Chinamen."

I just stare at him. What a snoop. Melvin thinks I'm silent because I want to hear him talk more. He doesn't know I'm trying to figure out how to make him shut up without hurling him into the river.

"You don't know who that guy was, do you?" he sneers. "That Chinaman is Old Man Wong. He's dangerous. He'll poison you with opium and diseases you never even heard of. Stay away from him, for your own good. I'm warning you."

"Don't be daft," I say. "He didn't hurt me. He gave me a fish."

"Don't eat it. Ask anyone. They eat weird food. They're not like us."

I pick up my fish and walk around Melvin to the house. I'll take it to Irene at the hotel and ask her to cook it for dinner. This is the first time I've seen Melvin away from his mother and the first time I've heard him say anything. What a pity that the words I hear him say are so stupid. When I write my play about coming to Calgary, I'll have to name one scene, "London Girl Meets Melvin the Idiot by the Bow River."

~

Two days later, I am sitting with Mrs. Brown on the front step of the house, tired from moving the first bit of furniture around. Tired from cleaning the place top to bottom. Tired from the excitement of it all. "We did it," Mrs. Brown announces to the little brown gopher nearby. "What do you think of that? And the next priority has to be school, young lady. Enough of this 'holiday'!" She laughs at her little joke, then takes my hand and sighs. "I couldn't have managed this week without you, dear," she says. For a long time, we sit on the step, looking at the river. "I'm sure that the Brantford house will be sold soon. Of course it will," she adds.

This day should feel wonderful. In some ways it does. But it also feels sad. Mrs. Brown is missing Reg and Mr. Brown a lot. She sighs deeply again, and keeps holding my hand.

Melancholy. That's the word for the feeling that comes to you after someone you love dies. You sigh a lot when you feel melancholy. Today is Good Friday, a strange name for the day the Romans killed Jesus. Good Friday is a sad day, and so I think there is no use trying to cheer up. We can save that for Easter. This is a good day to think about sad things and to wonder why peaceful people should be killed. I think about what a kind man Mr. Brown was and how he was beaten up. I do not try to cheer up Mrs. Brown. I think the best I can do is sit quietly beside her. And so I do.

Our goal is to have our work done so that we can sleep at the house on Easter Sunday. Easter is a day for celebrations and new beginnings, so we decide it's the best day to move. The last of our furniture and belongings are delivered on Saturday, and we spend the day making our beds and settling in as best we can.

Sunday morning we put on our best clothes and walk to Second Street to the Methodist Church. Like so many buildings here, it's quite new. We sing my favourite Hallelujah songs and hear the story about women going to the grave of Jesus to look after his body. But when they arrive, the grave is empty and an angel is waiting there. I've always wondered what it would be like to see an angel.

After church we meet the Bennetts, Cushings, Watsons and Lougheeds, and Mrs. Brown is invited to join the Temperance Ladies. Lorraine Hartry introduces herself to me. "Will you be in my grade?" she asks. "When are you coming to school?" I think maybe starting school Tuesday won't be so bad after all; the whole town isn't full of bullies and Melvins.

After our first real dinner at the house, we sit on the porch steps to have tea and look at the river. It has been a good day, but

I know Mrs. Brown is thinking about Mr. Brown again. "You won't believe what I saw the first time I went down on the river path," I say. She stares into space and doesn't answer. Maybe she can't even hear me. I keep talking anyway. "I was walking along the shore and I saw a red fox carrying a rabbit in her mouth. She was going to feed her family in a den in the bank!"

Mrs. Brown swings her head around and looks at me sharp; she's with me again. "Really? Where? Show me." And we walk down to the bank in front of the house, through the trees to the stony shore, and that's where we find him. He is lying face down on the stones, not moving. His fishing pole lies broken on the stones. It is Mr. Wong.

Mr. Wong

His left leg is bent impossibly. Mrs. Brown lifts her skirts and rushes down the bank. I feel frozen stiff. I can't tell if he is alive or not. His fish bucket is overturned, the water spilled; a dead trout lies on the stones. I walk down slowly. I stand the bucket upright and carefully place the fish back in it.

"He's alive," Mrs. Brown says, gently holding her hand on his throat. "Quick, run for the hatchet and a blanket. Bring the first aid box from under my bed, and some dishcloths." I race up the path to the house, my heart beating fast. *Please do not die.*

When I arrive back at the river, Mr. Wong is sitting up. His eye is swelling, a bruise is coming up on his chin and his lip is bleeding. He looks dazed.

"Cut two poplars as big around as your arm and taller than you are," Mrs. Brown says. She continues gently placing her hands on Mr. Wong's arms and legs, asking, "Does this hurt? Does this hurt?"

He is an old man, maybe around forty. It is clear his leg is broken. Mrs. Brown straightens it gently, puts wads of cloths along it, places a stick between his legs and ties them with rags to hold them still. We make a stretcher out of the blanket and poplars, help him onto it and carry him to our house, stopping to rest every now and again. Mr. Wong is not a big man.

We place the stretcher on the floor and quickly make our settee into a bed; then I run for a doctor. It will be dusk soon. I race along the path, over the bridge and into town. I know that the doctor's office is in his house on Atlantic Avenue; I've seen his sign. The doctor opens the door himself and quickly hitches up his buggy. He is used to emergencies, I guess. When I tell him what happened, he suggests we stop at the police station to report it. Soon we are crossing the bridge again. The sun shines gold as it reaches for the distant mountains.

Dr. Macy doesn't say much, just sets the leg, all business. Mr. Wong doesn't say a word when the doctor pulls on his foot to straighten the leg, but it must have hurt terribly. When he's finished, he says, "It's a clean fracture. He'll be good as new in a few weeks." He pauses and looks at Mr. Wong's swollen face, then at Mrs. Brown. "I suppose you can look after the rest?"

"Of course!" Mrs. Brown says.

"Are you planning to keep him *here?*" he asks.

"I hadn't got that far in my thinking. I was merely responding to an emergency." I can hear ice in her voice; she doesn't like his tone. She gets two dollars from her purse and pays him.

The doctor nods. "You should probably get him out of here right away. Good night to you." And he leaves us, closing the door firmly behind him.

Mrs. Brown puts salve on Mr. Wong's face and is busy making tea when the policeman arrives. He pulls out his notebook and pencil and asks Mr. Wong to tell his story.

"I am fishing," he says, "and from the bush some boys jump on me, break my pole, tell me, 'Go back where you came from.' They push me, call names to me. I fall and my leg go snap. I bang my head. They run away. This nice lady and girl help me."

"It isn't the first time," the constable says, "and it won't be the last, I guess. Some people think the Chinese bring trouble here." Mr. Wong looks at the floor. Constable Daniels doesn't notice, just closes his notebook and puts it in his pants pocket. "Some people don't like them mingling with the whites."

"He wasn't mingling," I say, "he was fishing. I've seen him there before. All he does is fish, and wave if you come by. He gave us a trout last week." I feel too embarrassed to look at Mr. Wong.

Constable Daniels stands. "There was a riot against the Chinese six years back—" he begins.

Mrs. Brown cuts him off. "That's enough," she says.

The constable doesn't say anything to that, just strokes his moustache and looks around the room. Looks at the gingham curtains in the window. Looks at the braided rug on the floor. Looks at the white pound cake on the table. And sighs. "Your husband…?" he asks.

"He passed away," Mrs. Brown says.

"I'm sorry." Now *he* is embarrassed.

Mr. Wong says, "Not to worry. I go soon."

"I think, with that leg, you should stay a while. You've had a shock. You cannot work in the laundry anyway. We can take care of you, Mr. Wong. Please stay. We have plenty of room here. You are welcome."

I can see that Constable Daniels wants to say something to stop this, but I can also see that he doesn't want to contradict Mrs. Brown. He nervously twirls his cap.

"You'll go to Chinatown and let Mr. Wong's friends know that he is here," Mrs. Brown tells him. It isn't a question. He stands, puts on his cap, wishes us good evening and goes out into the last of the Easter night.

Mr. Wong lies back on the white pillow. He is tired. "I have not money to pay house. No. I mean, I have not money to pay *rent*, I so sorry," he says. Then he suddenly smiles at us with his poor, swollen lip. "Just a few days maybe, you so kind. In springtime, I come back and plant garden for you. And I catch more fish for you."

Mrs. Brown has a thoughtful look on her face. She says, "It is better you just rest now. Please do not worry anymore, Mr. Wong."

And that is how the idea of a boarding house was born.

≈

"Gwen!" Mrs. Brown says the next morning. "If we got some lumber at the Eau Clair Mill and made the two upstairs bedrooms into four, and if we turned the storeroom into a bedroom for you and me, it could work. I'll talk to the landlord today. Maybe eventually we could even buy the place! What do you think?"

What I think is that Mrs. Brown looks more alive than I've seen her since before Mr. Brown was beaten. Her eyes sparkle as she sketches a floor plan on a scrap of paper.

"At church, Mr. Watson said, 'whatever we can do...' well, we need lumber, a carpenter to make the partitions and put in the doors. If we get three or four boarders it would be enough to keep us going."

Tuesday afternoon the work begins. Mrs. Brown doesn't care that I have postponed school for another few days. I take care of Mr. Wong, prepare meals and move furniture out of the way so the carpenters can work. I also go to Chinatown to find Mr. Wong's friends. I deliver a note from him with amazing writing on it. When I look at the note, I can't even tell which way is up and which way is down! I would like to learn to write in Chinese. It is beautiful and mysterious.

Mr. Wong works in a laundry and lives in a small wooden house with three other laundry workers near the railway tracks. I deliver the note to Mr. Wei. He writes a note while I wait, surrounded by the smells of soap and hot irons and spices.

That evening, Mr. Wei comes to visit Mr. Wong. After that, there is often one of his friends in our house. They bring us gifts; too many, Mrs. Brown says. They bring bags of rice, sweets, a chicken plucked and ready for the pot, or maybe some herbal tea. It is easy to see they miss women and children. They spoil us like crazy.

We tell Mr. Wong a little about Brantford, and he tells us his story. "I left my wife and baby daughter in China," he says. "Now she is not baby. I came to Canada to work on railway. But in 1885, railway was finished. Soon I have no job.

"I dream to bring my wife and daughter here, so I work hard to make money. But, there is never enough money to do it. My daughter is older than you now, Gwen.

"I dream to have a market garden like in China. There, people came many miles to buy medicine plants and vegetables. I grow good food. In summer I will grow good food for you, Mrs. Brown."

Mrs. Brown explains to me that the government wants to stop Chinese people from coming to Canada. They make them pay a lot of money called a "head tax." Every time Mr. Wong saves enough to pay it, the government raises the tax even more.

"Year after year," Mr. Wong says, "I try. Year after year, I have not enough money. I cannot." He bows his head for a moment. "She would be like you, Gwen," he says. And he flashes a smile that squeezes my heart and makes me miss my own dad.

By the end of the first week, Mr. Wong is up and hobbling around on a crutch he's made from poplar limbs. It has cloth padding for under his armpit. Once he can hobble out to the porch, he puts himself to work. While I fetch, carry and hold things, Mr. Wong repairs the porch steps and adds a willow railing.

Work on the house progresses, inside and out. The days become warmer. Flocks of Canada geese fill the sky as they migrate north. I want everything to stay like this, but I know it will come to an end soon, and it does.

"Would you like me to go with you to school tomorrow, or would you rather go alone?" Mrs. Brown asks one morning.

"With only a month until the holidays, is it worth it to even start?" I ask. Mrs. Brown laughs, and I heat the irons on the stove so I can press my school dress for the morning.

Central School is new, and Mr. Saretsky seems friendly and funny. At the first recess, I see Lorraine and her friends. "Why did it take you so long to start school?" she asks.

"I've seen you around," says a girl named Helen. "How did you get to stay home?"

Melvin's been lurking close by. "She's been busy with a Chinaman," he announces. "He lives with her. *And* she's a Home Girl," he adds. Melvin has said this to impress three boys. One wears spectacles, one is tall and one wears a tweed hat; the bullies from the store. They begin to laugh. I decide to leave so that I can go away and plan Melvin's funeral. I spend the rest of recess in the toilet.

By the end of the first day at school, I am trying to think of a way to make it my last. I stop by the general store to pick up a new latch for the outhouse door that Mrs. Brown asked for. The three bullies are there.

"Oh, the new girl is here," says the tall boy.

"Ewwwww. Make sure you don't get any Home Girl cooties on you," laughs Tweed Hat.

I pay for my package and slam the door on my way out. Grand Mary is sitting on the porch, as usual. The boys follow me onto the porch. "Hey! what did you buy? Chinese tea for your friend?" sneers Tall Boy.

Suddenly Grand Mary stands up. She's taller than you would imagine when she's wrapped in her blanket sitting on the ground. She stares hard at the boys, opens her arms like she's a great angel. *"Boo!"* she yells. As one, they take off down the street like they were shot from a sling shot. "Little savages," Grand Mary says, "just trouble." She winks at me and laughs, and I laugh, too.

∼

Mr. Wong is building a beautiful outdoor table. For the top, he has cut willow branches and nailed them into diamond and square patterns. It is almost finished. He takes the nails out of his mouth and asks, "How is school?"

I tell a lie. "Lovely, Mr. Wong, just lovely."

In the evening, after the carpenters have gone, we take our chairs outside and drink green tea around the new table. Before long, Mr. Wei and Mr. Sing come by to visit and play backgammon. At dusk, Mrs. Brown brings out two oil lamps so we can keep reading and they can keep playing. It is a warm night and we stay out until the moon rises. The gentle rumble of the men's voices adds to the evening symphony of magpies, robins, Canada geese and distant coyotes. Farther downriver, we can hear drumming.

The next night, we have visitors of a different kind. A hail of stones against the side of the house makes me sit up straight in bed. I hear a yell, followed by the sound of running feet. Mrs. Brown is at the door before me. I arrive in time to see three figures race across the yard and disappear into the ink black Prairie night. "China-lovers!" yells one. And then the only sound is the fire, hungry to burn the porch steps.

Warning

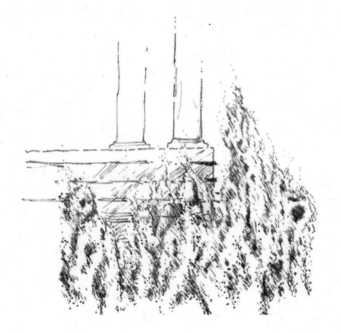

Mrs. Brown pumps frantically; I race with pails of water to Mr. Wong and he hurls them into the fire. The flames dance in the breeze, throwing light on his sweating face. It takes six trips back and forth from the well to the fire before the blaze is defeated.

Mrs. Brown kicks at the charred sticks. "There wasn't much fuel to keep it going. I guess they thought the porch would catch fire next." She shudders and looks out into the night. Across the river, a few lights twinkle in town. An owl hoots in the distance.

"You sleep now. I will sit and watch," Mr. Wong offers. "In case wind comes up and we missed a spark. It would be bad to have the fire start again." He takes a chair and sits outside on the porch and we return to bed.

As I close my eyes, I decide that this play will be called, "London Orphan Helps Defeat Wild Fire." I am too tired to think what I will do if I ever find out who started that fire.

I had thought that I could stay in bed a little longer because it's Saturday, but just after dawn, I wash my sooty face and run into town to the police station. It is a grey day. The clouds are dark and the wind from the north is picking up.

Constable Daniels comes a second time. "Getting to be a habit, young lady," he says, trying to be funny. I am too tired to laugh. Mrs. Brown has built a crackling fire in the stove; Mr. Wong pours four cups of green tea.

The officer sets his hat on the table, gets out his notebook and writes down everything we can tell him about the stones and the figures running away and the fire. Then, with his eye on the raisin pie I'd baked yesterday after school, he says he'll "get right on it." Mrs. Brown takes the hint, cuts him a piece and pours a cup of tea.

Constable Daniels finishes his pie, sits back on the hind legs of his chair and pats his tummy. "The way I see it, Mrs. Brown, you're a sitting duck out here. Just a little too removed from town. Anyone can come along the river bank and walk right into your house, even. There's all kinds of mixed blood people who live along the river, just east of here. There's all kinds of Treaty people in and out of town, nothing much but time on their hands. And of course, there's the eastern drifters and the ones from all over tarnation who are heading north to the Yukon gold fields." It's quite a speech he's making, I think. "It's not like being in Brantford, Ontario, you know." He doesn't know what happened to Mr. Brown, of course. And he has no idea how brave Mrs. Brown is.

She pours more tea and waits silently, listening. The constable keeps talking. "As an example, take the case of Charcoal. They had to track him down and hang him. Happened in Fort Macleod just last year. And then there was that nasty business of Almighty Voice over in Saskatchewan. Took a hundred men to kill him."

"What did he do?" I ask.

"He killed a cow for his wedding reception," interrupts Mrs.

Brown. "I read about the case back east in the *Mail and Empire.*"

"That was in the newspaper all the way out in Ontario?" Constable Daniels asks. He whistles softly. "But the thing is, Madame, people can't go around killing cows."

"What are the people supposed to eat if the buffalo are gone?" I ask him. Now I know that "The Cattle Thief," Pauline Johnson's story-poem, wasn't something she made up. It's true.

"Regardless of all that, Mrs. Brown, I'm suggesting that it may not be safe for you and Gwen to continue living here alone. There's been three cattle killed just over on Nose Hill, you know."

"It only takes about fifteen minutes walk to town. There's the ranch, and there are some houses along the Edmonton Trail. It's not like we don't have any neighbours at all."

"But aren't you afraid of being here without a man?" he asks.

Mrs. Brown's face turns red. "Mr. Wong is a man," she says. There is ice in her voice again, and this time the officer hears it. For a moment he is silent.

"Sure, but, what I mean is…I'm sorry, but he's likely the cause of the problem. People don't like strangers around here much."

"Strangers?" Mrs. Brown asks.

"You know what I mean," he says. "Foreigners."

"Oh, I see. You mean the 'foreigners' who built the railway that everyone is so proud of? The 'foreigners' who wash dirty English clothes in a hot laundry, or make large bequests so a public hospital can be built here?" Mr. Wong looks out the window. I bite the inside of my cheeks to stop from laughing. Poor old Constable Daniels suddenly looks like his underwear is too small. "And as for a man? Thanks very much, but most of them eat too much and aren't worth the trouble!"

The constable stands up, confused. "I best be on my way, ma'am," he says, turning suddenly and knocking over his chair. When he bends to pick up the chair his hat falls on the floor. "I'll certainly report back to you in a couple of days. Meantime, I'll just look around for some tracks. Mr. Wong? Would you mind showing me your shoes so I can see the difference between the culprit's footwear and your own shoes?"

"His tracks are the ones with the crutch mark beside them," Mrs. Brown says, rising. "I'm sure you won't have trouble identifying them. Good day, constable. Thank you for your manly help." She opens the door. Constable Daniels has no choice but to walk out.

Mrs. Brown closes the door and bends over double, her hand holding her laugh inside her mouth. Mr. Wong hides his face in his hands; his shoulders go up and down with laughing, and I giggle until the tears come. After a few moments, I see Mrs. Brown looking at the photograph of Mr. Brown that hangs above the table. I know that not all her tears are from laughing.

Mr. Wong says, "Better I go now."

"But your leg has not healed. You're welcome to stay here as long as you like."

"You are kind. I like it here. But it is time I go back to work. They need my help at the laundry. The constable is right. People don't like me living here."

"I like you living here," I say.

He touches my hair lightly. "Thank you."

A big silence comes into the room then. It seems so unfair. When I grow up I will not let bullies push me around.

"Even if you must go, Mr. Wong, please stay until after lunch," Mrs. Brown says.

But by the time we are finishing our beef soup, the wind is so strong it makes our house moan. And then, amazingly, it begins to snow. Great wet sheets of snow swirl around our house, blanketing the buds on the wild rose bushes, burying the remains of the little fire in our yard and piling up on our windowsills. We add wood to the stove and stare out the window in disbelief. Tomorrow is May Day! In Brantford, the daffodils will be blooming.

But Mr. Wong adds a log to the stove and laughs. "Welcome to Calgary," he says. "Not worry. It will melt soon." And he is right.

The next morning, an arch of clouds spans the western sky and a strong wind blows. We are all looking out the window. "Now you see what I mean. Look! The snow is half gone already. The wind is warm. This is the famous Chinook wind," he explains. "Warm up everything."

We spend the day taking away the charred bits of the porch and repairing the fire damage. Then I walk over to the Chinatown laundry, stepping around the puddles. I tell Mr. Wei everything that happened and how Mr. Wong is ready to come home again. Mr. Wei smiles sadly and says nothing. Mr. Wong's leg is still not good enough for him to hobble all the way home, so we hire a horse and cart.

After we get Mr. Wong up the stairs and into his house, he speaks to Mr. Wei in Chinese. They talk back and forth, back and forth and then look at me, smiling.

"What are you talking about?" I ask.

"You will see," says Mr. Wong. "You come here Tuesday after school. Then you see."

On Monday I am feeling lonely for Mr. Wong, and sad. But Mrs. Brown has a surprise for me after school: mail.

A big package sits on the table, wrapped in brown paper, tied with white string. It is addressed to *Mrs. Christine Brown and Miss Gwen Peters, Calgary, Northwest Territories.* We spend the evening reading letters from friends in Ontario. It is a feast for the heart. There is a letter from Maggie at the Girls' Home in England. Maggie was our house mother in charge of twenty of us girls in Hyacinth cottage. There's one from Mrs. Bostwick, our neighbour before dad died. There is one from little Pet who got adopted by people in Ontario, and one from Molly, my best friend. She sent her Gran's recipe for gingerbread cake, my favourite, and asked a million questions. Finally, there's a letter from Tim.

Tim and I were friends in London and he taught me to read. Now he's in Dawson City, Yukon, looking for gold. "I climbed the Chilkoot Pass, Gwennie! I was so high up I thought I'd meet God. But hard! I carried a pack as big as me. When I strike it rich I'll come to find you. Write to me." And I do.

When I stop at Mr. Wong's the next day, he is sitting on a stool folding laundry with Mr. Wei. He smiles, then puts his fingers between his lips and whistles. In answer, I hear thumping and yipping from under the porch.

Mr. Wei disappears and returns carrying three wiggly gold and white puppies, followed by the mama dog. "You like a puppy?" Mr. Wei asks.

I've never owned a dog, of course. My heart skips a beat. "I already ask Mrs. Brown," says Mr. Wong. "All you must do is choose. Happy Birthday tomorrow, Gwen."

I am overwhelmed. It's hard to choose, but I finally pick the pup that has white freckles on her feet.

I walk slowly through the downtown, carrying my golden puppy inside my apron. I will be fourteen tomorrow, right on the line between being a woman and being a little girl. I like this in between time. I like this life. And I like my little dog. I name her Chinook, after the warm prairie wind. I think that it's a poetic name for a dog on the Prairie.

"What you got?" asks Grand Mary from her place on the general store porch. I show her. "A good dog is worth a lot. You train her up good, Gwen."

The closer I get to the house, the more slowly I walk because I haven't thought up an excuse to stay home from school tomorrow, and I cannot imagine leaving this puppy. I'm already in love with her.

"But what will they think of me if I let you keep missing school? They'll have the truant officer after me. You leave Chinook with me; she'll just sleep anyway."

At recess, Helen says, "We heard there was a fire at your house. What happened? We heard you keep a Chinaman in your house. Why?" Melvin doesn't say anything, but he is standing with other children, listening, staring, waiting for me to answer. I feel like a plucked chicken on display in a butcher's window.

If her questions had been asked privately, and if she was asking because she wanted to be my friend, maybe I would have given her a decent answer. But she's just snoopy. "If you can't say something nice, don't say anything at all," Maggie used to say. I don't answer.

"Miss High and Mighty," sneers Helen. "Then don't answer. You think you're better than all the rest. You're not. You're just a Home Child with a bad attitude." Before the recess bell calls us back, I am at my seat, counting the minutes until it is time to go home. And this play will be called, "London Girl in Calgary Battles Blazes at Night and Rude Children at School."

I listen with half my brain to the arithmetic lesson. When it ends, Mr. Saretsky says something interesting. He says that last June was Queen Victoria's Diamond Jubilee—sixty years a queen. "All over the British Empire, celebrations marked this joyous anniversary. However, in Calgary, celebrations were marred by the terrible flood on the Bow River. So this year, we'll celebrate the queen's sixty-one years on the throne." I'm curious to know what his idea of celebrating might be.

"We're putting on a grand concert," he says. "When Hull's Opera House opened five years ago, the first performance was a concert put on by school children. We'll do that again. We'll do it big!" Then he rings the bell to dismiss us and leaves the room. It's the first good thing I've heard at school so far.

On the way home, I stop at the *Calgary Herald* office to drop off the boarding house advertisement that Mrs. Brown wrote. We're almost ready for business. I also go to the general store to buy black paint for our boarding house sign. Grand Mary is sitting on the porch, as usual.

"Hello, Grand Mary," I say. She smiles and nods, but suddenly ducks, her hand flying up protectively in front of her face. I turn around and see Melvin and the three Bully Boys disappear around the corner. Grand Mary touches her forehead and looks at the blood on her fingers.

"What happened?" I ask. Grand Mary just shakes her head and looks away. "Grand Mary?" But she doesn't answer. When I come out of the store, she's gone.

I run home and find Mrs. Brown sitting on the porch with Chinook on her lap. "I confess I didn't do much more than play with this pup all afternoon. I really did mean to have the curtains sewn and the wood chopped by now," she laughs. Chinook half falls, half jumps off her lap and runs to greet me. "I did manage to get to Linten's Book Shop however. Happy Birthday, Gwen dear!" She holds out a card and a book, *Beautiful Joe: An Autobiography of a Dog* by Marshall Saunders. Inside I read, "Dearest Gwen, You are sunshine in my life. Thank you. Love, Mrs. B."

"The author is actually a woman called Margaret. Everybody is talking about this book. I hope you like it," she says with a happy smile. "We could read it in the evenings by the fire like we used to, if you like." I would love that. I will also love to read another book written by a woman!

"Now, off you go, dear, no more work for you today. Dinner will be ready in an hour."

"I'll take the pup for a little walk by the river," I say. "Come, Chinook," and she follows as I run along the shore of the Bow.

I stop near the fox den to see if the kits are around, but Chinook keeps going. Suddenly, the father fox springs out of the willows and lands in front of the pup. She yelps as the fox swishes his massive tail, turns and trots up the bank. Chinook follows and in a moment they are both lost to my sight. I do not know whether to be afraid or not. Would a fox hurt a pup, lure her into the bushes and kill her? Would he play with her, or just lead her away from the den? I run up the bank and hurry along the path, but I cannot see them.

"Chinook? Come back!" I begin to feel afraid. What if she's killed? What if she drowns in the river? I follow the path east for what seems like a long time, but I cannot see them.

Around a bend, the man steps onto the path so suddenly I almost run into him. "*Oki!*" he says, "You're in a hurry. Why are you here?" He is so big he seems to block out the sun. His brown eyes flash down at me. His long black hair is bound in two braids decorated with leather strips, shells and beads. He wears a red wool blanket coat over his white shirt, dark pants and beaded moccasins.

I cannot find my tongue to answer.

Second Thoughts

"Who's there?"

The voice is a woman's but she is hidden by the man's great size. Suddenly he turns aside and Grand Mary is standing in front of me. She is chuckling.

"Oh you, Big Tom! Look what you've done. You've scared the girl half to death. I told you about her. *Tansi,* Gwen. Come on. I've got your little pup having her dinner. When I saw her, I figured you'll be along soon. Would you like something to eat, too?"

I am still standing like a statue on the path. My heart hasn't gone back to its normal beat yet. "Sorry," the giant says. "I didn't know you were a friend. But, you should be careful where you go alone. There could be danger in the hills around. Come on, Mary makes a good gopher stew. And there's bannock and tea if you like."

I follow him a few paces around the trees and into the camp site. They have a teepee here, and a big black pot hanging from a tripod over a fire. Even though I've never been in an Indian camp, I feel at home. It seems familiar.

Chinook is licking the last of her dinner from a tin plate and looks very pleased with herself when she sees me. I pick her up and sit on the grass near Grand Mary. She serves me like I am a queen, or at least a grown up: tea, warm bannock and gopher stew. Delicious.

"I would like the recipe for gopher stew," I say.

Grand Mary smiles. "I would rather give you a recipe for buffalo steak or roast duck but I guess it will have to be gopher, since that's all we seem to eat these days. And fish of course."

Grand Mary's forehead has a little bump where Melvin's stone hit her. She sees me staring and touches it gingerly. "It's alright, Gwen, not so bad," she says.

Big Tom eats in silence, but I can see he is alert to the sounds around us. He is not like anyone I have ever met. I can see that I can learn a lot from him if he will teach me. I would like to know how to walk through trees silently, like he did. That play will be called, "London Girl in the Prairies Learns to Move Like a Shadow on the Pathless Prairie."

I know Mrs. Brown will be worried about me so I shouldn't stay long. After I eat, I thank Grand Mary, lift Chinook into my arms and say goodbye. "You could use this," Big Tom says, and gives me a rope made from leather. It is beautifully woven; I've never seen such a thing.

"He makes all kinds of ropes," Grand Mary says proudly, "all different sizes, most for the ranchers and cowboys. It's for your dog until she learns to obey you."

Walking home, Pauline Johnson jumps into my mind. And that's when I realize why Grand Mary and Big Tom's camp seems so familiar. On one of the first pages in *White Wampum*, there is a drawing of a river flowing west to the setting sun. In front of that are trees, and in a clearing there are teepees, a fire, and people eating and talking near it. I saw that page for the first time three years ago, in London, on my eleventh birthday. Dad gave me the book just before he died.

I remember staring and staring at that picture, wondering what it would be like to be there. Who were the people? I wondered, and what would a wood fire be like with sparks flying free? What would that air smell like? What river was it? What were the people talking about?

When I met Molly and William at the school in Brantford and learned that they lived on the Reserve, I thought maybe they lived in a teepee like in that picture; that's all I knew about Native people. I didn't even know there were different nations then. When I told Molly that I thought she lived in a teepee, she laughed. She lives in a big farm house with red geraniums on the porch. But now, here in Calgary, it's like I stepped into the pages of Miss Johnson's book.

Mrs. Brown is sitting on the river bank, head down. Something is wrong. Why isn't she looking up? She is crying. "Mrs. Brown?" I touch her shoulder lightly.

Half of her hair has escaped from the bun and is blowing in the breeze. Her face is red; tears sparkle on her cheeks. She wipes at them with her apron. "I was worried about you, Gwen," she says. "I was afraid something terrible had happened." I put my arms around her, something I have never done before. She takes a deep breath. "I'm sorry, Gwen. I shouldn't have brought you to this wild and terrible place. They were right in Brantford. I shouldn't have done anything so quickly. I should have stayed there, where I knew people."

She sits up straight. She looks angry. "I should have stayed at least until the house sold. I should have stayed until the trial was over. I should have waited to sell the horse and got a better price. I should have looked for work first." She blows her nose on her hankie. "There is no point in both of us trying to live in this godforsaken country. I think I should send you back to Ontario, back to the Home, where they can place you with a decent family."

Deep inside me, I know that Mrs. Brown is missing Mr. Brown right now, so I don't say anything. When someone you love dies, sometimes you just want to give up; things seem too hard. That's what it was like for me after my dad died.

Mrs. Brown is not finished being angry. "I put two loaves of bread on the windowsill to cool this afternoon. I went to get my sewing, and when I came back the loaves had disappeared. Thieves! I cannot imagine the lecture Constable Daniels would deliver if he found out. What have I done, coming here to this wilderness?"

She fiddles with her handkerchief, ties it in a tight knot and looks out at the river. "And then I was afraid that you and the pup were drowned in the river or trampled by a wild cow or were carried away by wild people..."

I still don't say anything, because I am the child and she is the adult. Besides that, I'm not sure what to say. I'm not sorry we came. I like being with Mrs. Brown. I think Mr. Wong is wonderful, and so are Grand Mary and Big Tom. Maybe even Constable Daniels won't be so bad after he gets to know us a little bit. Of course, there's no hope at all for Melvin, but maybe some of the other children at school will be alright after a while.

And then I think about Ruth in the Bible again. "Whither thou goest," I say out loud. "Ruth." Mrs. Brown looks at me sharply, like she's just come awake. Chinook leaps up on her lap. "I'm sorry I was so late and that you were worried," I say. "Grand Mary is going to give me the recipe for delicious gopher stew."

"What? We can eat those little things?" And then Chinook leaps up and licks those tears right off her face and wiggles all over her lap and so Mrs. Brown can't help herself. She begins to laugh.

In the house, I tell her all about my adventure in the trees. I show her the picture in *White Wampum* so she can see what I mean. "Only there are not eleven teepees there, only one." And after that, we seem to be back to normal. Before bed, Mrs. Brown paints the sign: *Brown's River House—Bed and Board.* By the time she lays down her paint brush, she is humming.

In bed, I write a long letter to Molly. I wish she was here with me to share this adventure. I tell her all about the river, and Grand Mary and Big Tom and stupid Melvin and the fire and Mr. Wong. I tell her about Chinook. I ask her to hug her granny and grandpa, her parents, William and her little dog, Ji Yip, for me. I go to sleep dreaming that Ji Yip and Chinook are in a canoe taking Molly and me on an adventure.

When I wake up, I decide that I will be in the concert with the rest of our class to celebrate our gracious Queen Victoria. Maybe planning for that will help to make the next month at school more bearable.

Lessons

All of May was filled with rehearsals, catching up on school lessons, planting the garden with Mr. Wong and trying to get Chinook to obey me. We also got our first boarder.

At the end of the month, Mrs. Brown got another telegram to say that the house had not sold yet, but not to give up hope. "We will be okay," Mrs. Brown said, "and when it does sell, we will have the money to buy this house." Mrs. White wrote a letter saying that the police had still not found the last two criminals. But the whole month of May was not as busy as the first Saturday night in June.

Maybe it was the full moon that woke me. Or maybe the wind was blowing from the southwest and that's why I could hear the crunch of their feet on the river stones. Or maybe Chinook heard them—it's her licking my face that gets me up. Or, it could have been Mr. Dunn upstairs, our first boarder. He snores like a steam engine. I'm still half asleep as I bend to lace up my boots. I throw on my sweater and close the door quietly so Mrs. Brown doesn't wake up. It is very early in the morning; dawn has not quite arrived.

Chinook squats in the grass, then picks up her ears and looks west along the river bank. I hear them now, too, muffled voices laughing. Then, "Push off, push off, idiot!" I cannot see anything down there. I inch closer to the bank, strain my eyes to see. Chinook follows, hoping we're going for a walk.

"Melvin, you dunce! Where are the paddles?" I know who it is now. The big boys from school, the Bully Boys, the ones Melvin's always trying to impress. I hear footsteps running on the gravel, but toward me this time. The canoe rounds the bend and comes into view; the three Bully Boys are in it. Melvin is running along the shore, waving his arms in bewilderment and horror.

"We'll kill you for this, Melvin!" says Spectacles, standing up and dangerously rocking the canoe back and forth.

"Sit down, stupid idiot! Sit down!" cries Tall Boy.

The current catches the canoe and spins it around in slow motion. The canoe moves farther from shore, out into the cold, green water that runs all the way from the snow-capped Rockies to who knows where. Melvin is close to me now, but he doesn't see me, he's watching the canoe. He's half dancing, half running in panic.

I run back to the house and yell, "Mrs. Brown! There are boys in a canoe without paddles. Help!" And then I race down the path faster than I've run in all my life. Through the bush, past the fox den, along the poplar and willow-lined path to Big Tom and Grand Mary's place in the clearing. They heard me coming and they are already at the river's edge when I arrive, watching the canoe gather speed in the middle of the Bow River. It looks wider in the light of the half moon. Scarier.

Big Tom gives one end of a rope to Grand Mary and she anchors herself near a tree. He takes the other end with him as he splashes out into the icy water. Poor, fat Melvin arrives in time to watch with me as Big Tom lunges for the canoe. He is tall and strong, but the river pushes against him and it is hard for him to keep upright. The water is up to his neck. He misses his footing and is suddenly swimming. He lunges again as the canoe swings away from him in the current. He finally manages to grab hold of the side.

Spectacles reaches for the rope and makes the canoe teeter dangerously. "Keep still!" roars Big Tom, but it's too late. Tall Boy tries to correct the rocking, slips over the side and under the water. The canoe bounces up and down from the force of Tall Boy's exit. Big Tom disappears for a moment and then resurfaces, holding the boy by the scruff of his shirt, like a dog holds her pup.

Still holding the rope, Big Tom makes a grab for Spectacles' outstretched hand. Tall Boy holds the edge of the canoe and kicks hard toward shore. Even from the river's edge I can see that his eyes are bulging out of his head with fright.

Big Tom manages to hold on to the canoe and swim with one arm, but the current wants to pull him downstream. Now the rope is taut. Grand Mary holds on tight, an anchor in the terror of this early dawn. She is a mountain of strength.

"Help, Melvin!" I shout, and we grab the loose end of Mary's rope. The three of us pull together, hand over hand, until the canoe scrapes bottom by the shore. The two boys jump out and stand in the shallows beside Tall Boy, all of them dripping wet and shivering. Melvin stands near me. Tom pulls the canoe up on shore with one hand and then flips it over by the willows, back where it belongs.

"We should run," says Spectacles quietly.

"Maybe he'll kill us," whispers Tall Boy.

"My mother is going to kill me, even if he doesn't," Melvin says.

Grand Mary turns and walks to the clearing, and Big Tom motions for the boys to follow her. They are all shaking. I pick up Chinook and follow, too. Big Tom's face shows no emotion—not anger, not anything. He pauses calmly by the embers of the fire in the circle of stones. A great puddle of water forms by his moccasins.

Mary adds three logs and stokes the embers until the fire is blazing. She lifts the lid on the iron pot hanging there and stirs. She pours water from a bucket into a blackened kettle and puts it over the fire to boil. She gets a blanket for Tall Boy and drapes it over his trembling shoulders.

Big Tom motions the boys to sit, then disappears into the teepee. The boys squat miserably on the ground and wait for whatever will come. No one says a word. Chinook glances at the boys, then walks over and sits down by Grand Mary. The silence grows long as the sun rises up and up, making shadows appear and disappear until the clearing is bathed in sunlight. Grand Mary stirs the pot again and asks, "You like some gopher stew?" Chinook wags her tail and tilts her head like she's hoping that she understood that offer correctly.

"Yes, please," I say.

"Gopher stew?" whispers Tall Boy. "That's disgusting."

Grand Mary ignores his rudeness, lifts the lid and ladles me a bowl full. She carefully places a spoonful on a tin plate, blows on it to cool it, then offers it to Chinook. I see Spectacles sniff the aroma. He watches hungrily as the pup licks the plate clean. Big Tom is taking a long, long time to change his clothes.

The silence is so thick that the crack of a breaking twig sounds like a gunshot. Mrs. Brown and Constable Daniels come into the clearing just as Big Tom comes out of the teepee wearing dry clothes. Grand Mary graciously serves tea, sugar, canned milk and bannock to everyone. Except the Bully Boys. They don't seem hungry, and Melvin does whatever they do, even though it is clear he is starving. He must know that it's hopeless to try to impress them now.

"Looks like you been fishing already this morning, Tom," Constable Daniels says, gesturing to the four boys. "Caught a few big ones in the river, I understand. What are they? Big mouth bass?"

Big Tom puts his head back and laughs deep from his belly.

"Next time I'm going to get me a big net," Grand Mary says. "Too hard to haul them in with just a regular line!" And she laughs, too.

"Everyone safe?" asks Mrs. Brown, "That's the main thing."

"Only because Big Tom was there," I say. "I don't even know where this river ends up. Where would they have gone?"

"Into Cree territory," Big Tom says, "on a long, winding trip."

Constable Daniels puts down his tea mug. "What I want to know is what we are going to do next," he says. "The law was broken this morning by you four culprits. You stole Big Tom's canoe, and that's a criminal offense. On top of that, he had to risk his life to save yours. What do you have to say for yourselves?"

Steam is rising from Tall Boy's clothes as the fire warms him. The boys look into the fire, embarrassed, frightened, humiliated. They say nothing. They don't look like Bully Boys now, just scared kids. "My mother's going to kill me," moans Melvin.

"Shut up," hisses Tweed Cap.

Big Tom pours himself more tea. "The way I see it, it's up to the boys to figure out the next step." He settles down on the ground and gets comfortable leaning against a log. "I got all day to wait," he adds, and he stretches out his long legs and gazes calmly into the fire.

"Well," says Constable Daniels, standing, "maybe I'll just leave you then, and come back a little later, shall I?"

"Suits me," says Big Tom. "Do you mind, Mary?"

"I always enjoy a little company," Grand Mary says.

Tall Boy leaps to his feet. "Don't leave us here!" he shrieks.

Constable Daniels turns. "Don't worry," he says, "I'll let all your parents know where you are, and that you're safe and sound with Mary and Tom."

Mrs. Brown, Chinook, Constable Daniels and I leave then. "Grand Mary and Big Tom seem like kind people," Mrs. Brown says. "Do they live here year round?"

"Sure. They know how to." Constable Daniels tells us that they sometimes work on ranches in the area, but they always come back to camp by the river. They don't like to be away from here too long.

"Why?" asks Mrs. Brown.

"Because their son is at a Residential School in Red Deer, and their daughter is at a Residential School in Edmonton. They want the kids to be able to find them when they get out."

The constable explained that a Residential School is like an orphanage.

"But if the parents are alive, why would the kids have to go there?" I ask.

"Government rules," he says. "It's the law." I have many questions to ask about that, but I keep quiet. We have to go back to the house to make breakfast for our boarder, Mr. Dunn. He is a newcomer from the east, and we have a lot of things to tell him about how we live out here in Calgary.

~

That night, Mrs. Brown and I have just finished the dinner dishes when Chinook barks to tell us there's someone in the yard. It's a whole bunch of someones: Melvin, the Bully Boys, Grand Mary, Big Tom and Constable Daniels. "My, my!" says Mrs. Brown, "it looks like a whole delegation!" We pour tea for everyone and sit on the porch. Chinook checks to see if Grand Mary has any treats in her pockets, and she does: dry meat.

We all sit and watch the pup in silence. Then Grand Mary nods at Tall Boy. "You first," she says.

Tall Boy puts down his tea cup and stands in front of us. "I have something to say," he begins, and his face flushes red. He clears his throat. "It was us who threw stones at your house and started the fire. It was stupid. We're sorry. We want to know if we cut fire wood for you for the whole winter if you would forgive us." Mrs. Brown doesn't say a word, just nods at him. He sits down again.

Next Spectacles stands up. "We were mean to you, Gwen. We're sorry. We would like you to be our friend, if you'll have us." Now I feel my own face turn bright red. I don't want people to be mean to me, but it doesn't mean I want to be particularly friendly! I don't know what to say, so I say nothing and wait to see what will happen next. Spectacles sits down.

Melvin and Tweed Cap stand up next. "It was us who hurt Mr. Wong. We didn't mean to." Big Tom clears his throat, and Melvin gulps. "I mean, there is no excuse for what we did. What we did was terrible. We will apologize to Mr. Wong and see how we can make it up to him. We are going to the laundry now."

I am torn between wanting to cry and to laugh. What happened? It's like one of the miracle stories in the Bible. I look at Grand Mary to get a hint, but she's not looking anywhere except at Chinook, gently stroking the sleeping pup on her lap. I look at Big Tom, but he is looking out at the river, like he isn't even paying attention.

"I guess that's about it then," Grand Mary says eventually. She puts the pup down gently and stands up. "Your tea is very good. Thanks."

One by one, the boys go to her and shake her hand. "Be good boys," she says.

They shake Big Tom's hand and say, "Thank you."

Melvin asks, "Big Tom, would you come with us? Please?" Then the four of them follow Big Tom down to the river, toward the bridge and Chinatown.

"It's up to you if you want to lay charges against them," Constable Daniels says, "Mr. Wong could lay charges, too." He touches his hat smartly and strides away to catch up with the others.

When everyone has gone, Mrs. Brown and I have another cup of tea on the porch. "Now I know why they call it 'the wild west'," Mrs. Brown says.

As darkness falls, the stars become visible. We sit for a long time in silence. "Sometimes," Mrs. Brown says, "I can hardly believe that this is my life. It's so different from what I dreamed—even from what I imagined six months ago."

"I know what you mean," I say. I am looking for the North Star. "The first Christmas after my Dad died, I remember standing in my nightgown at the Home, looking out the window. I missed him terribly. I remember wondering if he had become a star and was watching over me."

"That's a beautiful thought, Gwen."

For a long time we sit quietly together and look at the sky. In the distance, a coyote howls. It is a beautiful sound.

The Longest Day

School is completely different now. The concert has changed everything. It's almost too bad it's nearly over for the year, just when I'm feeling more at home. Helen and Lorraine turn out to be friends, both at church and at school. The Bully Boys actually watch out for me and are nice to me. Even stupid old Melvin is practising being a human.

Last week, when I was delivering posters around town advertising the school Jubilee concert, I saw the Bully Boys talking and laughing with Grand Mary at the store. Once, I saw Melvin carrying a bundle for her.

The Bully Boys have already got a pile of firewood cut for us; we've always got lots of wood for cooking and baking. We'll be warm as toast if winter ever comes, and in the meantime, we are loving summertime here.

Mr. Wong's leg is as good as new now. He's making me a fishing pole and says he'll teach me to cast for trout just as soon as school is out. He's also helping us plant the garden. He's put in seeds his wife sent over from China. He says we're just going to love *bok choy*.

We are getting out early today, but still, I can hardly wait for the sound of the school bell. Janey and her mum are coming into town and staying overnight so they can come to the concert for our gracious queen at the Opera House. It is very hard to sit still for Mr. Saretsky's instructions about how the class will form two rows and walk together and all that. I know the drill already. I just want school to be over so I can run home and see if Janey has arrived yet. I don't want anything to spoil this whole long day. And it *is* a long day, the longest in the whole year, June 21st. It's called the Equinox.

Finally, school ends. I run like the wind through town, across the bridge and along the path. They are all on the front porch, watching for me. When Janey sees me coming, she jumps down off the porch steps and runs to meet me. She has already met Chinook, and the pup comes pell mell down the steps behind her. I cannot wait to show Janey everything. Mrs. Williamson and Mrs. Brown are already talking like old friends at the table with brownies and cups of tea. They look as happy to see each other as we do.

I show Janey the bedroom that I share with Mrs. Brown. I feel so proud to show her the little shelf above my bed because it's a place of honour: on it are the three corn husk dolls that Molly's gran made just for me.

Janey picks them up and examines each one, looking at the delicate beige leaves that have been crafted into beautiful dolls. They are light as feathers. They look like a grandmother, mother and daughter. "Oh," says Janey. "Could we show these to Mum? I can hardly believe such beautiful dolls can be made out of corn leaves."

We go out to the porch where the women are still drinking tea. "Molly's granny must think you are special to make these for you," Janey says.

When I start to talk about what it was like to visit Molly's family on the Six Nations Reserve, the story comes rushing out of me in great waves. I tell about how scared I was, and how lonely I was at school until Molly and William played with me and invited me to their home. I had never been on a farm; I'd never been invited to sleep overnight. "My first Canadian Thanksgiving was at their home. It was so much fun with feasting and stories and laughing. We were all there—baby Reg, Mrs. Brown, Mr. Brown…" I stop suddenly because thinking about the Browns makes my heart squeeze tight. For a moment, no one says a word.

"Those were happy times," Mrs. Brown says slowly. "And we were so happy to have Gwen in our family. She is a great help with the baby. She was a great help, I mean. And then in the spring this year, it all changed."

Janey sits forward in her chair, listening. "My husband was furious about the liquor being sold on the Reserve, and the stolen timber sales in Brantford, where we lived. It had been going on for years and it was hurting the people. The Mohawks were being cheated. He got together with some community leaders in Brantford and on Six Nations to find a way to bring the culprits to justice."

Mrs. Williamson says, "It's alright. You don't have to tell us the story if it's too hard."

"It *is* hard," says Mrs. Brown, "but you are the first friend out here I can talk to about it." And she keeps right on talking. She tells how Mr. Brown was warned to stop "interfering." She describes the night Molly's father found him in a ditch and brought him home to us all bloody. She tells how he became ill and then how baby Reg got sick. She tells about the night Dr. Evans touched her shoulder, removed his spectacles and said, "I'm sorry, dear. I'm so sorry."

She ends the story by telling about our departure from Brantford. And there is silence then, because we are all using our handkerchiefs. For a while, the only sounds are the sweet songs of chickadees, magpies calling and the wing beats of a pair of mallard ducks as they circle to land on the river.

"You are brave, Christina," said Mrs. Williamson.

Janey asks, "What was he like?"

"Funny!" we both respond, and laugh.

"He was gentle and a good father," adds Mrs. Brown. "He was kind and knew how to do things with his hands, like mend the horse harness and plant a garden."

Our story is set free in the west now, and that makes me feel more at home. "Come see our garden," I say. I take everyone to the fenced-in plot to see the potatoes, carrots, onions and turnips—and Mr. Wong's *bok choy*—already reaching for the sun.

The next best thing on my list to show Janey is the fox den. This play will be called, "London Orphan Becomes a Real Westerner."

Janey has a million things to tell me, too. "Cousin Wilbur

taught me how to ride a horse and how to put on the saddle by myself. It was a very humbling experience. I didn't know that horses would hold their breath when you pull the cinch. Then, when you get on, they let out their breath. That makes the saddle swing around and you find yourself upside down under the horse! I didn't know that horses could play jokes!"

We are laughing at the thought as we walk down the bank to the path. She lowers her voice even though there's no one but the magpies to hear her. "I even wear trousers sometimes at the ranch! Mama let me put on a pair of Wilbur's old ones. You can't *imagine* how much freedom you get wearing trousers!" she says.

I'd already decided that I likely won't be a corset lady, except when I'm performing on stage, but I never thought of wearing trousers. "Do you think you could bring me a pair the next time you come into town, so I can try them?" I ask.

"Sure. Now where's this fox den?" We walk along the river path, Chinook trotting along after us. But all that remains are a few old duck feathers and chewed up bones in the dirt mound in front of the hole. That smart mama and papa have moved.

Next, we decide to hunt for wildflowers to make bouquets for Mrs. Brown and Janey's mum. We turn and walk the other way and eventually climb up the bank of the North Hill. It's very steep, and I have to grab hold of the prairie grass to help me up. We're out of breath when we reach the summit, but it feels like a victory. From the top, we can see the whole town spread out before us. It's the first time I've ever been this far from our house.

The old Fort Calgary barracks, the Inglewood settlement, the hospital, the lumber mill, churches, opera house, stores, livery stable, Chinatown, humble homes and mansions are laid out like a scene in a picture book. Nudging the city both east and west, we see a few teepees with horses grazing peacefully nearby. To the west, the snowy peaks of the Rockies catch the sun. We can make out, far in the distance, the road to the Morley Indian settlement and Cochrane, the road that leads to the ranch where Janey lives. The railway follows the river coming down from the mountains, past a small herd of deer, a ranch and a large herd of cattle. I point out the railway and river east, and we remember our arrival at the station such a short time ago.

We sit down to rest. "Do you think you will stay here forever?" Janey asks.

"I hope so, I like it here." The air smells like summer; beside us prairie crocus, wild rose and woodland violets nod in the breeze.

As we watch, Chinook amuses herself by darting after bright-eyed gophers. She doesn't know yet that catching them is a hopeless cause. Gophers are too quick, too clever, and have front and back doors to their homes. She keeps trying anyway—until she spots the red fox. Then she is racing wildly down the hill, trying to follow the zigzag movements of the clever fox.

"Come on!" I cry, and we, too, run zigzags through the buffalo grass, our pounding feet releasing more summer scents into the air.

Suddenly, Chinook disappears. We stop our descent and wait for her to appear again. The fox still runs in the distance, but there is no little dog following. "Where did she go?" I ask. "Where could she go?" There's nothing here but grass, not even bushes and trees to hide in. She's too big to fall down a gopher or rabbit hole. We are breathless and confused. The fox is long gone.

We sit down to think about this mystery, and then we hear a tiny yelp. Together we hurry toward the sound.

Darkness to Light

Suddenly, I'm suspended in air. It's like slow motion. I reach for the sides of the hole I'm falling through and grab fistfuls of grass. Like Alice tumbling down the rabbit hole, my feet hang in thin air. Rudely, I land with a plop, and roll over just in time to avoid being Janey's mattress.

"What happened? Where are we?"

"Are you hurt?" I ask. High above, light filters through the hole as dirt trickles down on us. Chinook's warm tongue finds my face. I feel around and touch Janey's arm. That is all.

We have fallen into a deep, black hole. I sit up and stroke Chinook to reassure her. Janey sits up and moves close to me. I can't see anything but that small hole of daylight above. I smell something, though. I smell the earth, and something sour, too. It's strange yet vaguely familiar, like a dream smell.

We are stunned and sit quietly, holding hands, trying to think what has happened. We were walking down North Hill in the buffalo grass. And then we weren't. I suppose we are in shock. There is dirt in our hair and in Chinook's fur, but we are not hurt.

Suddenly, we hear a muffled sound. But before we can call out, there is the sound of soil being moved, scraping. Is it a landslide? An earthquake?

And then we hear a man's voice, gruff. "Well, little brother, it looks like you can't do anything right."

"Don't start on me. I promise I'll get *this* right."

"It's your last chance. I'd have thought you'd learned your lesson when your robberies went bad. I can't believe you even slammed the door of a safe on your own finger. Idiot."

The voice is angry now. "I said, stop it. This is the last time I'll ever ask you for help."

We hear footsteps, the scratch of a match, the clink of a glass lamp chimney set on a lamp. We are too shocked to move or make a sound.

A placating third voice says, "Mr. McBride, we're very grateful for this fresh start. Really. And don't be too rough on your brother. The Brantford operation was good until that meddler Brown poked his nose in."

My heart nearly stops. Light from a tunnel spills into the room we are in. I give a warning squeeze to Janey's hand, and we try to make ourselves small.

"We warned him. Tried to scare him off, but it went bad." A silent shadow cast by the one holding the lamp leaves the tunnel and comes into the space where we are. Two others follow. The three men are opposite us in a large underground room. One raises the lamp. Instinctively we crouch lower. I hold Chinook close, praying that she won't bark or whimper.

"It doesn't look like much, but it's a living," says McBride. "We just need someone to look after the stills when we're away, run the liquor. If you can do that, keep out of sight, I'll let you two in on it."

The light reveals a room with boards going part way up the dirt walls. In the middle of the room there are four big vats, a tangle of copper tubing, wooden barrels, boxes of liquor bottles and bushel baskets full of grain. We shrink into the shadows and hold our breath as the third man smiles, revealing a shiny gold tooth.

"Well, count us in," he says. "It's great to do business in the golden west. You say there's a good business here, and that we can get double the money if we ship down to the Americans? What else are they hungry for, Mr. McBride?"

Without waiting for an answer, Gold Tooth continues. "This will be a nice new beginning for us."

"They say that the West is the land of opportunity," says Mc-Bride. "I daresay it's true. Let's just have a little toast and then shake hands on the deal, shall we, gentlemen?"

He pours three tumblers full of whiskey. "Fine whiskey, Mr. McBride," says Gold Tooth, burping. "Mind if I have another?"

My heart is racing; I can hardly breathe. I hope that they will leave before I scream. "It's a deal," says Gold Tooth. All three shake hands.

McBride says, "I hope I'm not making a mistake taking you two on."

Missing Finger downs his second glass. "You won't regret it, big brother. Just you wait and see."

The men slowly disappear into the gloom of the tunnel. The lamp is blown out. A distant door is set in place. We hear them shovel dirt against it. We're trapped; buried alive.

"Bloody." Janey's voice comes without a body and sounds loud in the dark. "Don't let go of my hand," she says, "or we'll never find each other again. We need a plan." The obvious one is to go back the way we came in.

Janey gets on her hands and knees and I stand on her back, but the hole-opening is much too high to reach. Then, I cup my hands and Janey tries to stand in them, but without a wall for balance we both fall down. We try to move some boxes to stand on, but that doesn't work either.

"If we can't go out the same way we came in," she says, "the only way out is through the tunnel. Bloody."

We feel our way, crawling along the dirt floor in the direction of the tunnel. We crawl slowly around sacks and boxes, bottles, tubes and baskets. Chinook follows. I turn around twice to see that point of light. I know we need to move diagonally away from it, so I use it like the North Star. I remember being in the woods alone at night. Seeing that star was a comfort to me. I try to think of the point of light in the same way. This helps to get us across the main room and into the tunnel.

Once in the tunnel, we are in complete darkness. We feel our way along, inch by inch, in that pitch black. I've never been in darkness like this before. I feel like crying.

But when I touch the wooden door, I don't feel scared any more. I feel angry. I stand and pull, then push hard against it. It holds firm. We pull again and again and nothing happens. We kick it. And then we sit down to think some more.

Suddenly, I think about how Melvin has a criminal for a father. I think about Mr. Brown and what he looked like after they beat him. I think about how weak he was after that and how he got influenza. I remember how baby Reg was sick and then sicker. I think about the funeral. I think about how terrible it is that these cowards would beat up Mr. Brown in the night, just for money.

Next, I think about how hard it is when somebody dies. And now I'm as angry as a storm. Now I have the strength of a bear. "Hold the dog and get back!" I roar. "This is for baby Reg and Mr. Brown. And even Melvin!" I shout into the darkness.

I ram that door with all the strength in me. How *dare* those men do their dirty business in Brantford! How *dare* those men come here to do more dirty business! I ram that wooden door again with all my might. My shoulder makes a funny noise, but so does the door. I've moved it.

Janey takes a turn next. She is yelling the names of Mr. Brown and baby Reg and Melvin, too, even though she doesn't know them. We batter and kick until finally the bottom of the door pushes out a little, so the top moves toward us. We push Chinook through the opening at the top and she begins to dig back toward us. Soon it's enough, and we can squeeze through, too.

Climbing out of that tunnel and taking that first gulp of fresh air feels like a miracle. Like the Lazarus story in the Bible, we were buried and now we're free. The wind on my face feels like a blessing. We make our way down the hill toward the path by the river. I want to run, but my legs feel shaky. I can hardly believe that we fell into a hole. I can hardly believe that Melvin's dad is a criminal. But mostly, I can hardly believe that we know who beat up Mr. Brown. Janey and I hold hands and walk along the river, trying to absorb all that information.

When we are still far from the house, we see Mrs. Williamson running along the river path, holding up her skirts. In the distance, Mrs. Brown stands on the bridge. Constable Daniels is half way up the hill behind our house. Chinook races on ahead, barking her happiness. Janey and I yell and wave to let everyone know that we are safe.

When we are all together at the house, the story comes pouring out of me like a volcano, all about how we fell down the hole, the still, how we heard the men talking about the Brantford operation and Mr. Brown. Then I tell them about the beating, the funerals, the train trip with Gold Tooth and Missing Finger, Melvin's dad, everything.

The constable writes it all down as fast as he can. When I finally stop for breath, he looks to Mrs. Brown. "Everything she said is true." He puts on his hat and whistles. "This is big," he says. "I will send a telegram immediately. Then I'll bring another constable so we can see the still."

Janey and I look a mess, of course, with soil and bits of grass and roots all over us. After Constable Daniels leaves, Mrs. Brown and Mrs. Williamson get hairbrushes and, without saying a word, they brush our hair. It feels so gentle, so beautiful. I cannot remember anyone ever brushing my hair before. Perhaps when I had a mother, she did it. But that was many years ago.

∽

We are almost ready to go to bed by the time Constable Daniels comes to report to us. Luckily for him, there are still plenty of chocolate cookies left from dessert. "We have been watching McBride for quite some time," he says. "We suspected that he was up to no good, but we didn't have anything on him. Until tonight. He was clever to keep his stills underground."

He helps himself to another cookie. "Our telegram to Brantford Police confirms everything you said, Gwen. I don't think that these three will be doing any kind of business except prison business for a long, long time. They were so confident, they didn't even bother to hide or keep quiet. They were having a partnership celebration dinner at the hotel when we arrested them. My deputy has them in custody now."

"Was Melvin there when you arrested them?" asks Mrs. Brown, alarmed.

"No, he didn't see his father arrested, I'm glad to say."

And this play will be called, "Home Girl and Dear Friend Fall into a Dark Hole and Bravely Bring Criminals to Justice." With the Assistance of her Brave Little Dog, of course.

Celebration

I am ready for this concert. My shoulder hurts from last night, and Janey and I stayed up talking half the night, but I am still ready. I don't feel tired, I feel happy. I stand beside the soft, green curtain with the other students and wait in the shadows. Janey and her mum are sitting in the front row with Mrs. Brown, Mr. Wong and Constable Daniels. There is a big crowd. Almost everyone I know in Calgary is here, except Gold Tooth, Missing Finger and poor old Melvin's dad. They are in jail. I decide that I will be especially nice to Melvin because it must be very difficult to have a father in prison.

Willie the caretaker is with us backstage. "I knew you'd be back for a real performance," he whispers. "Good luck!"

Mr. Saretsky gives us the signal that it's three minutes to curtain time. I hope none of the less experienced students will wet their pants, or panic and go silent. On the other hand, I've seen everyone rehearse their songs and recitations so often that I could just step in and do the whole show by myself.

Mr. Saretsky takes his place at the piano. Willie shuts off the electric lights in the hall and opens the curtain. Mr. Saretsky strikes a loud, strong chord. We file onto the stage and turn smartly to the audience. Mr. Saretsky strikes another chord, the audience stands as if they are one body and we sing "God Save Our Gracious Queen." I sing with all my new Canadian heart for our dear old queen back in England.

The audience sits and Mr. Saretsky walks to the centre of the stage. He opens his mouth to speak and then closes it again because a man's voice from the back of the hall rings out in the darkness. "Here now! I don't think you ought to be here. Excuse me. This is the concert for Queen Victoria. It's for...it's for..."

Everyone turns around in their seats to stare into the gloomy darkness at the back. "I know that," a voice says matter-of-factly. In the hush, we hear footsteps and then three people become visible in the lights spilling off the stage. A man is walking backwards toward the stage, trying to block the way of two others who are moving steadily forward.

Grand Mary has her eyes on the stage and is moving down the middle aisle toward us, like a ship at full sail. She moves with grace and purpose. In her wake comes Big Tom, walking silently and with dignity. The backwards man suddenly stops, bewildered and unsure what to do. Someone in the audience calls, "Let's start the show!" Another whistles. The backwards man shrugs and retreats.

Grand Mary and Big Tom sail to the front of the hall and pause. There are no more seats left. Big Tom sits on the floor near my people. Constable Daniels gives his seat to Grand Mary and joins Big Tom. "You can start now," Grand Mary announces to Mr. Saretsky. "We're ready." She smiles and waves to me. I wave back, even though in the real theatre you aren't supposed to do that.

A voice from the back of the audience calls, "Come on, let's get on with the show!"

"To the queen!" shouts another. "Let's salute the queen with the performance!"

"Hear hear!" cries a woman. "Let's begin!" People begin to clap and whistle. It feels like a party.

Mr. Saretsky raises his hand and clears his throat. "I am pleased and honoured," he says, "to introduce you to a fine group of talented young people from our public school. Our presentation is called, 'A Salute to Canada, in Honour of our Queen,' It is our tribute to a great country." There is applause.

"I would like you to know that our class voted that profits from the ticket sales will be given to the Chinese mission to buy Chinese-English dictionaries," he says. Mr. Wong winks at me and smiles.

The show is great fun, and no one forgets a word, a song or any of the drills, not even the youngest children. The class performs Canadian songs about lumberjacks and maple syrup and Rocky Mountains. Individually, we sing, dance a jig and recite. Mr. Saretsky gives a stunning solo performance, reciting all eighteen verses of "The Walrus and The Carpenter" from Lewis Carroll's *Alice in Wonderland.* He is very funny and I hope I get to have him for a teacher next year. I think he has a lot of potential.

When it is my turn, I walk out on stage alone and take a deep breath. I look at each member of my new family: Grand Mary, Big Tom, Mrs. Brown, Mr. Wong, Janey and her mum, and even

Constable Daniels. I know that they are on my side, cheering for me. Knowing this makes me feel good.

When I introduce the poem, I tell the audience about the famous Mohawk Canadian whose poems and stories have taught me what a real Canadian is. I tell the people about seeing her perform in London, England. "This is why I wanted to come to this beautiful land," I say.

Grand Mary waves her fingers at me and smiles. "*Hiya.* You tell it, Gwen!" she says loudly.

"I dedicate this performance to Miss Pauline Johnson."

The Song my Paddle Sings.

West wind, blow from your prairie nest
Blow from the mountains, blow from the west...
The sail is idle, the sailor too;
O! wind of the west, we wait for you.
Blow, blow!
I have wooed you so,
But never a favor you bestow.
You rock your cradle the hills between,
But scorn to notice my white lateen.

My legs aren't shaking one little bit. I feel the words of Miss Johnson come alive inside me as I see the Grand River in Brantford in my mind. I dance the words on the water, and they seem to rise on the wake and then land softly on the shore. Her words

are like music, like a painting, like a story in my heart. The magic
of them fills me.

I stow the sail; unship the mast:
I wooed you long but my wooing's past;
My paddle will lull you into rest.
O! drowsy wind of the drowsy west,
Sleep, sleep,
By your mountain steep,
Or down where the prairie grasses sweep!
Now fold in slumber your laggard wings,
For soft is the song my paddle sings.

August is laughing across the sky,
Laughing while paddle, canoe and I,
Drift, drift,
Where the hills uplift
On either side of the current swift.
The river rolls in its rocky bed;
My paddle is plying its way ahead;
Dip, dip,
While the waters flip
In foam as over their breast we slip.
And oh, the river runs swifter now;
The eddies circle about my bow.
Swirl, swirl!
How the ripples curl
In many a dangerous pool awhirl!

And forward far the rapids roar,

Fretting their margin for evermore.
Dash, dash,
With a mighty crash,
They seethe, and boil, and bound, and splash.

Be strong, O paddle! be brave, canoe!
The reckless waves you must plunge into.
Reel, reel.
On your trembling keel,
But never a fear my craft will feel.

We've raced the rapid, we're far ahead!
The river slips through its silent bed.
Sway, sway,
As the bubbles spray
And fall in tinkling tunes away.
And up on the hills against the sky,
A fir tree rocking its lullaby,
Swings, swings,
Its emerald wings,
Swelling the song that my paddle sings.

Listening to the applause wash over me like waves, I suddenly think about my dad. "Stories will carry you through, Gwen," he would tell me. "They are like rivers, carrying you along through life. It's a good thing to know good stories." I curtsey slowly and leave the stage. Dad was right.

At the end of the show, our class troops back on stage to sing our national anthem. I remember how embarrassed I was when I first arrived in Canada and didn't know the words to "The Maple Leaf Forever." I know them now, and I sing them with all my heart.

Afterwards, parents come backstage to collect their children. Mrs. Brown comes to collect me. Grand Mary, Big Tom, Constable Daniels, the Williamsons and Mr. Wong wait nearby.

"Very good, Gwen!" Mr. Wong says and bows.

Reverend Langford stops and shakes my hand. "Grand performance!" he says, "I hope you will read Scripture at church one day. You could liven it up, I think!"

Mr. Smyth from the *Calgary Herald* newspaper brings out his pencil and little notebook. He asks my age, how long I have lived in Calgary and where I learned to recite. He wants to know how it is I watched Miss Pauline Johnson perform in London.

"Mr. Smyth," I say, "It would take a bleedin' book to tell the answers to all those questions."

"Then perhaps I could come by tomorrow so you can start to tell it to me?" he says, smiling.

I turn to get my coat from the hook. Willie is standing there, wearing a very big smile. He turns to a woman behind him and says, "She's right here, ma'am."

She is wearing a blue hat with feathers and a blue dress made of silk that rustles when she moves. Even her satin shoes are blue. She looks exactly the way I remember.

"Miss Peters?" she asks. I am speechless. "My name is Pauline Johnson." I know that my mouth is hanging open, but I cannot think of what to do about it.

"I enjoyed your performance very much, dear," she says. "Would you and your friends care to join me at the hotel for a cup of tea?"

The End

Notes

Chapter 2

The death of Mr. Brown is based on what happened to Chief George Johnson, Pauline Johnson's father. He tried to stop timber thieves from stealing lumber from and taking liquor to the Reserve; he was beaten and left for dead in a ditch. He never fully recovered his strength and died when Pauline was 23 years old. Newspaper reports tell us that, "For Johnson's efforts to control the theft of timber and sale of alcohol on the reserve by unscrupulous non-native men, he was badly beaten in 1865. He was attacked again and shot in 1873." He died in 1884.

Chapter 3

The train left Brantford on Thursday, March 31 and arrived in Calgary at 2:30 am Monday, April 4.
da = yes (Russian)
Dominion Census: Population of Calgary was just under 4,000.
All of the poetry quoted here is in *White Wampum*, published in 1895. It is in the public domain.

Chapter 4

Hull's Opera House, built in 1893, had a capacity of 1,000 people. It was located at Centre Street and 6th Avenue S, just north of Knox Presbyterian Church.
The Langevan Bridge across the Bow River was built in 1892.

Chapter 5

The first Chinatown was located east of the railway station, north of Atlantic Avenue (9th Ave) in the early 1890s. The site contained a laundry, two restaurants, two grocers and a rooming house. In 1890 Chinese chef Jimmy Smith donated his entire estate to the founding of Calgary's first General Hospital. During a smallpox scare in 1892 an angry mob of 300 Caucasian men rampaged through Chinatown, ransacking businesses and assaulting residents. The Canadian government Head tax was in place in 1898.

Chapter 7

Margaret Marshall Saunders' *Beautiful Joe* is a classic story of a dog abused and rescued. *Beautiful Joe* was an award-winner and the first Canadian book to become an international best seller. It was published in 1893.

Chapter 8

Oki = Hello (Blackfoot)
Tansi = Hello (Cree, pronounce: dansay)

Chapter 9

On June 11, 2008, Prime Minister Harper made a Statement of Apology to former Indian Residential School students. He said, "the treatment of children in Indian Residential Schools is a sad chapter in our history." He acknowledged that this school system, where children were often forcibly removed from their homes and taken far away, was damaging. Many were inadequately fed, clothed and housed; all were deprived of their parents' care and community. Native languages and culture were prohibited. Some children died. More than 150,000 children attended Residential Schools. The schools were started in 1870; the last one closed in 1969.

Chapter 11

The girls falling into the still is based on a story told me by Violet, a woman I met years ago in Saskatoon, Saskatchewan. She gave me permission to use the story; it had happened to her.

The frontispiece in White Wampum:

To learn more about E. Pauline Johnson, visit:
www.chiefswood.com

To learn more about British Home Children, visit:
www.collectionscanada.gc.ca/

Thank You

At various stages, kind people helped with this manuscript.

Thank you Christine Pinkney, Calgary Public Library; Professor Donald Smith, Doreen Orman, Elder Barbara Sinclair Shoomski and May Wong Musters.

Thank you also to Mr. E. Wisherts for valuable railway information and to Lynn Odbert Matthison, Andrea Czarnecki, Marty Brown, Billie Brown, Claire McMordie, Gail Sidonie Sobat, Mary Kurucz, Allison Leam, Amy Chen, Marie Saretsky, Kate Saretsky and Melinda Lang. I am ever grateful to my editor, Jennifer Day of Toronto who is wise, firm and gentle.

Others who assisted were staff at Glenbow Archives, Brantford Public Library, Calgary Public Library, The Barnardo Homes and students at The Alexandra Writers' Centre, Calgary. Ivy Sucee and Hazel Perrier, also descendants of Home Children, have been unfailingly supportive.

Special thanks to Mr. Matthew Brown, Mission, BC. May you live a heroic, long and happy life!

Part of the proceeds from the sale of this book are donated to organizations that help children.

About The Author

Carolyn Pogue has written twelve books for children, teens and adults. She also gives talks on peacemaking, cultural understanding and children's peace camps across the country. She found inspiration for the *Gwen* series in the life of her grandmother, a Barnardo Home Child, and the life of Mohawk poet-performer E. Pauline Johnson. Carolyn lives in Calgary, her home base for frequent travel.